Mrs Capper's Christmas

Mrs Capper's Casebook #4

David W Robinson

© David W Robinson 2022

Edited by Maureen Vincent-Northam
Cover Design Rhys Vincent-Northam

No part of this book may be used or reproduced in any manner whatsoever without written permission of the author except for brief quotations used for promotion or in reviews. This is a work of fiction. Names, characters, and incidents are used fictitiously.

Prologue

Good afternoon and welcome to Christine Capper's Comings and Goings, your weekly video blog of what's been happening in Haxford, brought to you by Pottle's Pet Supplies, the only place your pets would shop if you gave them the choice and loaned them your credit card. Today I'm going to take you back to the week before Christmas, and that series of events which shocked us all. Do you remember the final few days in the run up to the festive break? The weather was awful, and I had a nine o'clock appointment at Haxford Public Library, but the attack on poor Benny Barnes, which created chaos on the High Street, was soon overshadowed by other, more shocking and potentially frightening events in the shape of the Graveyard Poisoner striking again… but I'm getting ahead of myself here. Let me backtrack to the morning of Tuesday December 21st, and a warning from Radio Haxford's Reggie Monk…

Chapter One

"... You're tuned to Radio Haxford with Reggie Monk, and that was Greg Lake telling us all about how he believed in Father Christmas. Didn't we all? Ha, ha, ha. It's half past eight on a cold and gloomy Tuesday morning, we have just four days to Christmas, and here's a bit of traffic news for you. You know that the news on Reggie Monk's breakfast show is always good, it's fun, it's upbeat? Well, this time it isn't. Ha, ha, ha. Sorry, folks, but if you're thinking of hitting town for some late Christmas shopping, then put it off. Police are warning of what they describe as a serious incident on the High Street in the vicinity of Benny's Bargain Basement. Someone must have found Benny's wallet. Ha, ha, ha. Seriously, Haxforders, the police tell us that the High Street is closed to traffic while they deal with the incident, and that means Yorkshire Street, Market Street, and Huddersfield Street are gridlocked. Is that one for your weekly vlog, Christine Capper? Ha, ha, ha. We'll press on regardless and what better way to pass the time in a traffic jam than listening to Radio Haxford and Slade wishing everyone a merry..."

Reggie's garrulous announcement hit me as a triple whammy. First and foremost, he mentioned me by name, second, would the incident, whatever it was, have any potential for my weekly vlog, and third, I had an appointment at the library at nine o'clock; would the traffic jam make me late?

Hands shaking, anxiety climbing towards panic levels, I looked through the window, saw no sign of him, so I picked up my smartphone, swept my finger over the lock screen, and hit the icon for my husband. While I waited for Dennis to answer I reconsidered my priorities. The library staff, all two of them, were expecting me, so that had to come top of the list. Re the incident's potential as a vlog post, I'd need a lot more information, and finally, it wasn't the first time Reggie Monk had mentioned me and my vlog on his breakfast show.

Picking up the call Dennis broke into my thoughts. "Hey up, lass, Reggie Monk's just mentioned your name."

I could imagine Dennis's features split apart by a wide grin. "Yes, I heard it too. Listen—"

"You're getting too well known, Chrissy. Time you were advertising Haxford Fixers on your fillums."

"Dennis—"

He interrupted me again. "I mean, it costs us a fortune to advertise in the Recorder, you know. If you could give us the occasional plug—"

This time, I cut in on him. "Shut up and listen, Dennis." When I was satisfied that I had his undivided attention, I went on. "You're supposed to be taking me to the library."

"I am. I'm on me way to pick you up now."

"Yes, well, Reggie Monk says the town centre is

gridlocked, so you'd better get a move on or I'll be late."

"Where do you think I am other than right in the middle of the jam?" He distanced himself from the phone for a moment to shout at another motorist. "And the same to you, pal. Get your missus to buy you a proper driving licence for Christmas." He came back to me. "Are you still there, Chrissy?"

"Yes, Dennis. I'm listening to you shouting at other drivers."

"Well, I wouldn't call him a driver. An aimer. That's what he is. I meanersay, how much road does he need for a—"

"Never mind your rants and tants. How long will you be?"

"I reckon five minutes, maybe ten."

"I'll be waiting for you."

I cut the call and glanced at the wall clock above the fireplace. While much of the surrounding area was already trimmed with tinsel and other Christmas paraphernalia, most of it reflecting the flickering lights of the Christmas tree, the clock remained barren, reminding me that I would need more tinsel and a stepladder to deal with it. A single strand draped over the top and hanging down the sides should do the trick or perhaps a garland with strands hanging down like theatrical drapes. If the clock's lack of adornment hogged my attention, it did give me the time as 8:33. I couldn't do it now because I was short of tinsel, and anyway I didn't have time. Not when I had to get to town which was allegedly jammed with traffic. I decided to attend to the clock later in the day.

I switched off the radio, turned the thermostat down a couple of degrees (neither I nor Dennis approved of heating the house to comfort levels when only Cappy the Cat was in residence) and checked my bag to ensure I had everything I was likely to need for the day. I left the front room for the hall where I spent a moment or two pondering whether to go for the knitted scarf and hat, or the dark brown coat with the fur-lined hood. Neither was particularly fashionable. For business appointments, I kept a small range of suitable apparel, from the formal and austere, sombre suits, to the more flamboyant and revealing skirts and blouses, but another glance through the window at a fast-moving sky threatening anything from rain to sleet to snow made fashion statements a non-starter.

I opened the front door and a strong blast of icy wind persuaded me. I would freeze in a thin suit, and any kind of hat would need pinning into place, so it would have to be the brown coat and hood. How fashionable did I need to be for an appointment with a stick in the mud like Alden Upley?

I could think of better ways of spending a bitterly cold, Tuesday morning. Curled up under the duvet would be top of my list, but an appointment was an appointment. Upley's assistant, Kim Aspinall rang me and booked the time, but she gave me no hint as to what she and her boss wanted, so with a few minutes to kill before Dennis's ETA, I put the matter to one side and considered the unspecified, serious incident on the High Street.

A small industrial town with a population of less

than 25,000, Haxford simply did not do serious crime. True, there was the Graveyard Poisoner, and he last struck about a month ago when his latest victim turned up in the grounds of St Cross church. He was a matter of concern for every man, woman and child in the town – especially the elderly men – but he had been about his evil business for the last two years and the police were no nearer catching him. Aside from him, Haxford was a strictly minor crime area.

Was I an expert on crime in Haxford? I was. Twenty-six years ago, I came to the end of my service as a police officer. No I didn't retire. I was only twenty-seven at the time. In fact, Dennis and I started a family. A good number of years later, I became a private investigator. Both callings had taught me that in the eyes of law breaking and enforcement Haxford was small potatoes. There were no major banks worth holding up, no large companies holding thousands of pounds in payroll money, and the bookies and the bingo hall tended to pay their big winners by cheque or direct bank transfer. There was nowhere worth robbing on the 'serious incident' scale, and it was too early for the Graveyard Poisoner to strike again. He tended to leave months between his crimes, and as I thought about it, over a year had passed between his last victim and the one before.

Of course the High Street incident did not have to be crime. It could have been a burst water main, a collapsed sewer or a ruptured gas main, but would the police be dragged into such matters? Traffic control only, I decided, and if that was the case, they would have made it clear to Radio Haxford. Whatever the serious incident, it had to be criminal, and for them to close the High Street there had to be a threat to the general public.

Was it possible that Reggie was exaggerating? He was well-known for his false laugh, and quirky, not very funny gags, but it would be a bit extreme, even for him, and anyway, hadn't Dennis just said he was caught in the jam?

Almost as I thought about my husband, his dirty, dark blue van trundled up the street and pulled up across the drive. Its windows were so covered in grime that I couldn't see through them, the wheel trims which were supposed to be chrome-ish, were black with muck and I could hardly read the legend 'Haxford Fixers' emblazoned along the side.

I stepped out of the house, closed the front door behind me and after checking that it was locked, I strode along the drive as Dennis climbed out of the driver's seat, walked round to the nearside and opened the passenger door for me.

"Could you not have come in your car, Dennis?" I asked.

He pointed up at a murky, turbulent sky which I believed would deliver snow before the day was out. "I don't like driving her in this weather. She's an old lady. She needs cosseting, cuddling, gently encouraging." He reached into the glove box and came out with two black, dustbin liners, spread one of them on the seat back, and the other on the seat itself.

"I may not be an old lady, but I need cosseting, cuddling and gently encouraging, too."

Dennis helped me up into the van. "You keep telling me we're too old for that kind of stuff."

"Let's just get a move on. If the High Street is as bad as you and Reggie Monk say, I'll be late for my appointment, and it's business, not social."

He closed the door behind me, made his way round the front of the vehicle, and climbed behind the wheel. Old and tatty the van might be, but the heaters worked and it was a good deal warmer than the outside.

Even so, I was determined to make my feelings plain. "If you got your finger out and got my car back on the road, you wouldn't need to come home and give me a lift. You've had it two days now. I mean, how long does it take to replace a headlamp and buckled wing?"

"I had a toil getting the parts."

Dennis started the engine, pulled forward across the road and with his head turning one way and then the other like a spectator at a long tennis rally, he checked both wing mirrors as he reversed into the drive, before driving out to the right.

"A toil?" I demanded. "You only had to go to the main dealers for them."

"It's in Huddersfield. And you ought to see how much they charged me for a headlamp and a bolt-on wing panel? I didn't pay that much for my car."

That was one of Dennis's exaggerations. His car was a 1979 Morris Marina which he found as a shell rotting away in a scrapyard, and he paid less than a hundred pounds for it. He spent the better part of a year rebuilding it with original parts, once again coming mostly from one of Haxford's several scrapyards. All up, he estimated that it cost him less than five hundred pounds to get it fit for the road. For all that I had never been a trained bookkeeper, I was the one who did his accounts and I was sure there had been some creative costings on his part. A good number of those spare parts were attributed to Haxford Fixers' accounts as 'sundry items'.

Whatever its pedigree, his precious Morris Marina was more comfortable than this noisy and unkempt (but nice and warm) van, but neither were as comfortable as my new-ish, compact Renault. When I thought about my poor little car, I wish that Chihuahua hadn't dashed across the road like that. It wasn't nearly big enough to take on the Rottweiler it was chasing. I had to swerve to miss the little dog, and I collided with a metal bollard on the side of the road. I was unhurt and so was the Chihuahua when it came scurrying back to its mistress' arms, but the car lost its nearside headlight and wing, and both Dennis and our son, Simon (a police officer) insisted it had to go in for repair, leaving me at the mercy of my husband's busy schedule.

"Geronimo did the paint job yesterday afternoon, and he's valeting it, as we speak," Dennis promised as he drove to the bottom of the cul-de-sac and turned left towards the town centre. Geronimo was the nickname of Tony Wharrier, one of his business partners. "Do you want it at home or somewhere in town?"

"Town, I think. Kim didn't say what they wanted and I don't know how long I'll be with them. Tell you what, send me a text when you're ready for bringing it back."

"Gotcha."

"Good. Now, tell me about this incident in town."

"Can't tell you nowt cos I don't know nowt, except the town's choc-a-bloc with cars and wagons, all going nowhere fast. Tell you what, though, there's a shedload of plod about, and according to Grimy, summat's gone off at Benny Barnes's place. Armed robbery, Grimy says."

The idea was absurd. "Grimy? Lester Grimes?" While Dennis half turned to shout at another driver, I vented my frustration. "I do wish you'd call your partners by their proper names, Dennis."

Concentrating on the road again, he defended himself. "Grimy's always been Grimy, just like I've always been Cappy and Geronimo's always been Geronimo. What else are you gonna call three bloke with names like Grimes, Capper and Wharrier?"

I was too interested in events on the High Street to be bothered with the debate. "So what does this High Street business have to do with Lester Grimes?"

"He saw it. See, he's late in this morning cos he's got toothache and—"

"An eight-pint toothache? I suppose there was karaoke at The Engine House last night?"

"He says not. He was on his way to the dentist and he was passing Benny's place when he heard the shots. Grimy reckons as it was him who called the cops and he was still there when they shipped Benny off to t'hospital."

The question and answer session ended there and

I stared anxiously at the busy road ahead, looking for hints of gridlocked traffic.

Haxford sat in a valley, and but for the area around Huddersfield Road, which followed the track of the sluggish River Hax, getting to the town was always downhill. My concern as Dennis negotiated Moor Road, was not so much getting into town – by now I was resigned to turning up late – but getting back later, when, as it seemed likely, we would get some snow.

"You'll be all right," Dennis assured me when I broached the matter. "Take it steady and you'll manage, but if you do get stuck, give us a shout and I'll come out with the wrecker and tow you home."

His promise reassured me. The wrecker, one of two vehicles owned by Haxford Fixers, was older than the van, older than Dennis's prized Morris Marina, but it was possessed of a four-wheel drive and I'd never known it bogged down no matter how bad the weather.

It was the council's proud boast that no one single Haxford resident lived further than ten minutes from the busy shopping heart of town. That might well have been true, but not at eight-forty in the morning with only half a week to Christmas, and certainly not when the police were out in force dealing with… an armed robbery?

"It's nonsense," I said as Dennis tagged onto a long queue where Moor Road met the town centre bypass. "An armed robbery at Benny's? He never keeps more than a couple of hundred pounds on the premises, and even that's only his float."

"I'm only telling you what Grimy told me. I tried

ringing our Simon, but he weren't answering. Ten to one they've got him on traffic control." Dennis applied the handbrake while the queue waited for the traffic lights to change. "I suppose you're gonna poke your nose in."

"I do not poke my nose in, and the police certainly won't entertain my services as a private investigator. But people do rely on me to give them the backstory on what's going on in Haxford."

The lights changed. Two cars got through then came to a halt on Yorkshire Street, the other side of the box junction, and Dennis put the parking brake on again. There were still four vehicles between him and the lights and I calculated that we had a good five minutes before we would get across the junction. Even then, we still had a hundred and fifty yards to go to the public library.

"You and your blinking blog. It's an excuse, that's what it is. Let's you carry on playing at being a copper."

"It's a vlog, not a blog. I do it on video, and I am not playing at being a police officer. I'm reporting, Dennis, telling people about Haxford. And I don't hear you complaining when the sponsors pay me."

"Oh, aye, I forgot about that. What was it Pottle's paid you last month? Fifty quid? I bet the taxman's rubbing his hands at the thought of his share."

The lights changed again and this time, three vehicles got through, but the third stopped in the middle of the box junction, preventing the crossflow traffic from moving.

"Another one found his licence in a bowl of

Corn Flakes," Dennis grumbled. He wound down his window, leaned out and shouted, "That box junction was a waste of yellow paint." He closed the window again and the offending driver gave him a single finger salute.

"Do stop moaning, Dennis," I said. "It doesn't get you anywhere."

"It lets off steam. I hate driving these days."

It wasn't the whole truth. Dennis did find driving on the packed roads a frustration, but underneath that angst, he was suffering withdrawal symptoms. A man obsessed with all things mechanical, taking Dennis Capper away from his workshop and toolbox was like separating a mother from her babies.

I checked my watch and read a couple of minutes to nine. "I'm going to be late so I'd better ring Kim and let her know. She won't worry, but you know how picky Alden Upley can be."

"Picky's the last word I'd use for him. He's a total pain in the—"

"Yes, Dennis, we know your opinion of him and anyone else who doesn't understand internal combustion engines. The minute you get the other side of the junction, drop me off and I'll walk the rest of the way. And when you see Lester, tell him I'll want a word after I'm through at the library."

Chapter Two

The moment we were across the junction we came to a stop once again, this time on the tail end of the next line of traffic, held up by the lights at the four-way junction of Yorkshire Street, the High Street and Batley Way a hundred and fifty yards ahead of us.

I didn't wait for Dennis to come round and open the door for me, but climbed out and with a final warning to get my car back to me ASAP, I closed the door and walked off along Yorkshire Street in the direction of those same four way lights.

As I strolled along, I rang Kim and warned her I was behind schedule. As ever, she took the news in her stride. "No problem, Chrissy. I'm not there yet, and I'll bet Alden is wetting his clean knickers. The perishing bus can't get through all this traffic."

Haxford Public Library stood right on that four-way junction at the heart of the jam but it was the other side of the road to me. Crossing would not be a problem. As Reggie Monk promised, the streets were gridlocked and it would be easy enough to dodge between the stationary vehicles. I nevertheless decided to walk up to the traffic lights on this side of the street. It would give me the opportunity to see what was really going on along the High Street. I did not, for one moment, believe Lester Grimes's tale of armed robbery at Benny Barnes's place, but even from this distance I could see a police officer, swathed in a lemon, high-visibility coat, preventing traffic from turning into the High Street, redirecting them along Batley Way – to the right – or straight further up or down Yorkshire Street to the northern or southern by-passes. As I neared the junction, I recognised my son and the smile crossing my features did not have to be forced.

If Simon Capper was a bit of a disappointment to his father (but not much) who had expected him to join the team at Haxford Fixers when he left school, he was a source of immense pride to me and I never tired of boasting about his progress. Not for him the mechanical iniquities of the automotive world or the intricacies of domestic appliances such as Dennis and his partners routinely serviced, repaired and occasionally sold. From school he did three years of university and when he got his degree, he followed in his mother's footsteps and joined the police service.

His sister, Ingrid, twenty-three now, lived with her boyfriend in Scarborough where she worked as a club and pub singer. We saw little of her other than during the summer when we would go over there now and then. We'd already had a card saying they were fully booked over Christmas and New Year, and they would not be visiting. I felt a little cheated by this. We got on all right and it would be nice to have her home for Yuletide, but they were a popular duet and I couldn't deny my daughter her shot at fame and fortune… even if, as was likely, it came to nothing.

Simon was an inch or more taller than his father's five feet eleven inches and had to bend to receive a hug and peck on the cheek from me and I took the opportunity to remind him, "You know you're all expected for Christmas lunch on Saturday, don't you? You and Naomi and Bethany."

"We know, Mother, and hey, it'll be a special celebration. One of the older sergeants is retiring and I've just been told that come the New Year, I'm moving to CID."

"And about time, too."

Twenty-seven years of age, married with a young daughter, Simon had tramped the beat around Haxford for the past five years and sat the National Investigator's Examination earlier in the year. A town as small as Haxford couldn't afford to promote him to CID, but with the retirement of a sergeant, there would be enough play in the budget. I glowed with pride. My son, the proper detective.

"I can see you making inspector or superintendent one of these days," I told him.

Simon, standing in front of a couple of police barriers preventing traffic from entering the High Street, acknowledged my opinion, and then moved into the road to explain the situation and outline the detours to an angry motorist. While he was dealing with the irritated woman, I took the opportunity to glance along the High Street.

From Yorkshire Street, it ran for about three hundred yards until it met Huddersfield Street, and there was an element of homogeneity about the area in that the shops, banks, and building societies on Haxford High Street could be found in any town or city anywhere in the country, albeit on a smaller scale in our humble neck of the woods. And, naturally, there were local businesses interspersed with the better-known names, places like Benny's Bargain Basement, Pottle's Pet Supplies, or Sonya's Unisex Hairdressing (where I was a regular customer). Under normal circumstances parking was restricted to fifteen minutes, return prohibited within two hours, except, of course, on bus stops and within the confines of the two pedestrian crossings where there was no parking at any time. During my eight years with the police, I lost count of the number of times I had to warn or book motorists for breaching the regulations. There was adequate parking behind the library and again off Market Street a couple of hundred yards towards the northern bypass, and in my view there had never been any excuse for laziness.

Normal circumstances didn't apply right there and then. Where Simon was guarding the Yorkshire Street end, I could see one of his colleagues carrying out similar duties at the Huddersfield Street junction, and except for police cars and a large, white, scientific support van, there were no vehicles of any description, not even buses. What was strange, however, was the number of people, ordinary members of the public, milling around. More uniformed officers were shepherding them across the street from the immediate vicinity of Benny's and the bank next door, and a white shroud had been put up in front of Benny's Bargain

Basement. As I watched, I could see officers, all clad in the familiar, hooded suits of forensic or scene of crime teams, coming and going. Across the street, a crowd had gathered outside Iceland and despite urgent pleas from the police, they were not for moving. I noticed some of the staff of a local estate agent's, easily identified by their sober business apparel, amongst the crowd. If nothing else the 'serious incident' provided excellent entertainment.

"What's going on, Simon?"

My son dropped an indulgent smile on me. "I can't tell you, Mum."

"You mean you won't tell me."

"We're all under orders to shut up." He checked his wristwatch and tried to divert my attention. "And what are you doing out? You know it's threatening to snow, don't you? Shouldn't you be at home rehearsing your vlog?"

"I've an appointment at the library at nine o'clock." I pointed to the building across the street on the corner of Batley Way.

He looked at his watch again. "You're ten minutes late. Come on. I'll see you across the road."

"I'm fifty-three, not ninety-three, and perfectly capable of getting across the street under my own steam, thank you. And you're being very mean to your mother. I only asked what was going on."

"What was it you told me when I first signed on? Learn which orders to disobey. Well, I learned, Mam, and this is one order I can't ignore. It came straight from Paddy Quinn." Simon laughed. "I don't think the inspector wants you poking your nose in."

I put out a convincing harrumph. "You're getting as bad as your father. I do not poke my nose in." I switched to pleading. "I'm a vlogger, Simon. My audience expects me to bring them up to date with all the news and they expect a more in-depth analysis than Reggie Monk gives them. How can I tell them what I don't know?"

"I can't tell you anything except that it's a serious incident. But I will tell you this. That mate of Dad's, that Lester Grimes, was the one who phoned it in."

"I already know that. Your father told me."

"Then quiz Grimy. At least that way, you keep me out of trouble."

"Maybe I will. Don't forget Saturday, three o'clock."

I reached up to hug him, peck him on the cheek a second time, and then made my way through the throng of traffic across the street to the library.

According to the foundation stone in the front wall of the building, the premises were gifted to the town of Haxford by the Barncroft family at the turn of the 19th/20th century. It's hardly surprising. The Barncrofts owned most of Haxford at one time and Benny Barnes, one of the town's most popular characters, often claimed he was related to them. He never backed it up with evidence and there was sufficient difference between his name and Joshua Barncroft's to cast doubt on the claim.

Built of stone, the library's high, vaulted ceiling did nothing to dispel the chill of a winter's day, and Dennis, who despite his obsession with engines, knew a thing or two about many different trades and was no slouch when it came to chasing up business, had made formal suggestions to Haxford Borough Council on having a suspended ceiling installed. He'd even offered them a price for the job. Not that he and his partners were builders or anything, but they would have sub-contracted it to professionals. In his pitch, Dennis reminded the council that not only would a suspended ceiling make the building warmer but it would also reduce the heating costs. The town hall had agreed to consider the proposition, a phrase which was easily translated as, 'no thanks'.

Putting on my best business front, I strode to the counter where I was greeted with a disapproving look from head librarian, Alden Upley.

"Good morning, Mrs Capper. A little tardy. Our arrangement was for nine o'clock."

"Have you seen the traffic, Alden?"

"I have. I left home early to accommodate it."

"I couldn't. My car is off the road. I had to wait for Dennis to pick me up. And I did call Kim to let her know I'd be a little late." I decided there was no point telling him I only rang Kim five or ten minutes ago.

"Ah. Sadly, Ms Aspinall is also late. Please forgive me. I assumed you had missed or disregarded Mr Monk's warnings on Radio Haxford."

I accepted his apology and allowed him to show me through to the staff room where I removed my coat while he switched the kettle on.

From the age of nineteen, I served eight years

with the police, and became acquainted with many people in Haxford, one of whom was Alden Upley. In a town where most men picked up nicknames – Cappy, Geronimo, Grimy, for example – he managed to gather two. Allez-oop was the more polite, but some of the library's reading room regulars, the bar flies as Kim Aspinall called them, tended to disregard his given name and often referred to him as, 'Up yours', frequently to his face and especially when he upset them.

A little older than me, somewhere in his mid-fifties, he had been a fixture at the library for longer than most people cared to remember. For sure, he was there in the days when I walked the High Street beat, and that was going back over thirty years. For much of the last two decades he had been in charge. Kim and other assistants who worked there before her said he was never a bad boss to work for, but he did tend to the pernickety, and quite often the focus of his exasperation were those same bar flies populating the reading room. He was persuaded that they congregated there while they waited for the pubs to open. I knew those barflies well and I knew that Upley was probably right, but Haxford Borough Council's rules were quite clear on the matter. If they had a legitimate purpose in the library and were not causing any trouble, they could not be asked to leave. Legitimate purpose included reading the day's newspapers even if they were only trying to pick out the winners at Wetherby. It was those same barflies which probably persuaded him, if not the town hall, that the library did not need to be more attractive by becoming warmer, and I guessed that he was secretly glad when the suspended ceiling never came to pass.

The one thing Upley did not do was gossip, and while we waited for Kim to arrive I pumped him for information on the closure of the High Street. He remained as tight-lipped as Simon.

"I suspect a burglary," he announced, but even without the thin hints Simon had put my way, I knew differently. The police would not turn out in numbers for a burglary, and they certainly would not close the High Street for what was a common offence.

Equally bizarre was Kim Aspinall's opinion when she finally arrived at the library at half past nine, thirty minutes adrift of her official start time.

Kim and I were good friends, even though she was about eight years younger than me. My mother and hers were workmates as a consequence of which I knew the family well. Joan Aspinall left Haxford a good few years previously to move in with a man in Leeds and Kim settled down with a Haxford man… until it went wrong. During the relationship, which lasted about three years, she deployed typical, twenty-first century disregard for formality by not bothering to marry her partner. I couldn't argue. Dennis and I lived together for two years before we married, and we only went through with it when we learned I was pregnant with Simon.

Kim had worked as a clerk with a range of institutions before moving to the library a decade or more back, whereupon she demonstrated a complete disregard for the Dewey Decimal System, maintaining that sorting library books according to classification and then alphabetically by author was not that far removed from common or garden, alphanumeric filing. Beyond that, I knew that Kim was good with the customers; polite, helpful, and when confronted with the unreasonable, capable of dealing with it.

When I pushed her on the incident at Benny's Bargain Basement, Kim said, "While I was walking down Yorkshire Street from the bus station, I bumped into that mate of your Dennis's, that Lester Grimes. He reckons he was the one what called the cops. He says it's a terrorist do. And he must be right, Chrissy. Your Simon's on the corner stopping all the traffic and the High Street's shut and swarming with plod. I bet some of 'em are armed, as well. I bet they're on Iceland's roof, and watching for the terrorists coming out of Benny's. You used to be a cop. What do you think?"

"I think it's the most idiotic idea I've ever heard."

"Yes, but—"

"Use your head, Kim. Why would any serious terrorist organisation choose Haxford as a target? Worse, why choose Benny Barnes's place? It's not calculated to make politicians sit up and take notice is it? Besides, there are hundreds of people out there watching from the pavement. The police would clear the street if there was any danger of terrorism."

Upley delivered tea for us, and insisted that with the library open for business, we would have to gather behind the counter if we were to get down to negotiations, and as we left the staff room, the head librarian attended to the first customer of the day, while I advised Kim, "You shouldn't take too much notice of Lester Grimes. He's prone to exaggeration, especially after a night in the Sump Hole." People were not the only ones to pick up nicknames in Haxford, and the Sump Hole was the local soubriquet for The Engine House pub on Weaver Street.

Sorting out a pile of books for return to the shelves, Kim hastened to correct me. "He's got toothache and he says he wasn't in the Sump Hole last night."

"Yes, and Dennis whisked me away to a Pacific paradise last night, for a week of unbridled passion."

Kim's eyebrows shot up. "Did he?"

I couldn't help but laugh at my friend's naivety. "Did he heck as like. Dennis reserves unbridled passion for engines. Do you know, just for a laugh, I once said to him, Dennis, I have a secret lover. He takes me back to his place for an hour of lust every Wednesday afternoon. Do you know what Dennis said?" I put on a deep voice, mimicking my husband. "Oh, aye? What kind of motor does he drive?"

Kim laughed with me. "And did you? Have a secret lover, I mean?"

Once again, I had to wonder about Kim's occasional bouts of gormlessness. "Of course I didn't. Dennis might be obsessed with engines, but he's enough for me. And as for Lester Grimes… trust me, he was just trying to wind you up."

While Kim loaded the books onto a trolley and

took them to the shelves, I concentrated on Upley. "So, Alden, what seems to be your problem that you need a private investigator?"

"Theft, Mrs Capper. The theft of expensive library books."

Chapter Three

One dark and not so stormy night twenty-seven years ago, Simon Capper came into the world, and I spent the first few years of his life as a stay-at-home mum, but the moment he started school I felt the restless call of boredom. Money was never an issue. At the time Dennis and I got together, he earned excellent wages as a top-flight mechanic, which would eventually see him with enough capital to set up Haxford Fixers. So money was never the great issue for us that it was for so many. It was that feeling of imprisonment, of virtual house arrest, having nowhere to go during the day, no one to speak to; that's what I found difficult.

When Simon started school, I left my daughter, Ingrid in my mother's care, while I tried a few part time jobs, in shops, working the checkouts at CutCost (Haxford's largest supermarket), even a morning job tapping away at a keyboard and answering the phone in an accountant's office, but none suited me or my inquisitive restlessness. Frankly, I believed I was meant for better things. Returning to the police service was not an option. Attacks on the police were not as frequent as some of the tabloids would have readers believe, but they did happen, and I had two young children to consider. By the time Ingrid was born, three years after Simon, any remote idea the 30-year-old me entertained of life as a police officer was buried forever.

With the turn of the millennium and the growth of the internet to the point where it became one of the most important channels in most households, I set up a blog, Christine Capper's Comings & Goings, concentrating on life in and around Haxford as seen from the point of view of a small family. Twelve years on from the inaugural post, it remained one of the most popular blogs in the area, and over the last few years, as well as picking up a few local sponsors like Pottle's, like Sonya's, it graduated quite naturally from a blog to a vlog.

My hitherto unsuspected ability to dig out the stories of others for inclusion in the blog/vlog tempted me along another avenue, and I became a properly licensed private investigator. I had the necessary investigative skills, I had the necessary assertiveness, and of course, I had eight years' experience as an active police officer, but mind you, other than with the clients' permission I rarely included tales of my investigations in my vlog and when I did, I tended to keep names out of it.

I also tended to be choosy about the work I took on, as I proceeded to explain to our head librarian. "I don't deal with criminal cases, Alden, and theft is criminal. It's a matter for the police."

He was not dissuaded. "I am aware of that, but in this case, the thieves are stealing from the town hall, and by default, the council tax payers of Haxford. And we have spoken to the police to no avail. They gave us a crime number so we were able to claim the loss on the council's insurance, but our lords and masters at the town hall told us they cannot be troubled with claiming a few pounds. They did, however, insist that if we can pinpoint the culprits, the authority may very well decide to prosecute."

I tutted. What was it about this man that he could be so selective about what he chose to hear? Dennis had the same ability, and with him it was just as deliberate as with Upley, although, to be scrupulously fair, Dennis rarely listened to anyone or anything unless it concerned the mechanical intricacies of motor cars.

"Please listen to me, Alden." I numbered the items on my fingers as I carried on speaking. "I do divorce statements and photographic evidence of same, a bit of people tracing, usually families trying to track down a son or daughter after they've left home. I've done the odd case of heir hunting, which is people tracing again, and I occasionally help clients establish their innocence when the police suspect them of a crime, but that's about it. I don't even take on bad debt recovery, which a lot of private investigators do… although I can be persuaded to make an effort to trace debtors if pressed, but once again, that's people tracing, and I do not knock on the door. I simply pass the information to the person or company hiring me. I don't take on anything that might lead to confrontation with either the subject of the investigation or the police, and as such, I do not take on criminal inquiries."

"I hear you, Mrs Capper," he said with the

ineluctable air of someone who had heard but listened to nothing, "but I hardly think a thief concentrating upon library books is some kind of criminal mastermind, and anyway, our proposal would not entail confrontation of any description. We simply need you to identify – if possible – the miscreant and our superiors will deal with the matter from there."

He delivered the last line with an ominous gravity that reminded me of Marlon Brando reassuring Signor Bonasera that friendship with The Godfather would ensure that people feared him. I was tempted to ask whether the council would issue a warning in the shape of a horse's head in the perpetrator's bed.

At that moment, Harry Kepler and Rita Nuffield walked in. They constituted a brace of Kim's barflies. Both just the right side of sixty, both were unemployed. No one could remember when Harry last held down a job, but it was rumoured to be when the street lighting was still gas fired, and according to my sometimes wobbly memory, Rita's last gainful employment was as a tea lady at the town hall, a job she lost when they found she was helping herself to tea, sugar, and some of the goodies she was supposed to sell. By helping herself, I don't mean she was pinching the odd brew and biscuit. She was nicking the stuff packets at a time.

A face lathered in cheap makeup, she wore a pair of baggy pants and a quilted topcoat, while for his part, Kepler was, as usual, unkempt, unshaven clad in shabby jeans and a shabbier fleece.

As they entered the library, they turned right towards the reading room, but Kepler spotted me, and with a broad grin on his face, his uneven, ill-fitting dentures showing behind rubbery lips, he detoured and leaned on the counter.

"Hey up, it's Chrissy Capper. Working in t'library now, are you, lass?"

Upley looked down his nose at Kepler. "Not that it's any of your concern, Mr Kepler, but Mrs Capper is here on business."

"Not funny business, I hope." Kepler gave Upley a scathing look. "Not with you anyway." He transferred his greedy eye to me. "You want funny business, Chrissy, then I'm your man. Just say the word—"

I was a good deal less generous than Upley. "Go away, Harry."

"Ooh. Like that is it. If you're not working here, it strikes me you must be poking your nose in where it don't concern you. Eh? Are you still playing Capper the copper?"

At the door to the reading room, a broad grin spread across Rita's face. You'd think she'd be jealous. They were not officially a pair but I'd heard the rumours.

I narrowed my eyes on Kepler. "If you're not careful, Harry, you'll get a Capper the copper clout on the conk. Now go away and look at some stars."

Harry's wizened features screwed up further. "Why do people say that to me? Huh? They've been saying it for years and I still don't understand it. The only stars I look at are in the paper, and they tell me today's my lucky day. Yours too, Chrissy, if you play your cards right."

I clucked like an irritated mother hen. "How can you get to your age with a name like yours without having heard of Johannes Kepler?"

He thought about it. "Nope. Don't think I've got a cousin called Joanne."

"Johannes, you barmpot. Johannes Kepler was a seventeenth century, German astronomer and he formulated the laws of planetary motion."

Kepler shrugged. "Not one of our family, then. We're all from Haxford."

I fixed Rita with my gaze. "Take him away will you?"

"Where do you want me to take him? Huddersfield?"

"Just out of my sight." I switched my glare to Kepler. "For the last time, go away."

"Right. So you don't wanna know what I know about the barney at Benny's Bargain Basement?"

That got my attention. I pointed to the reading room. "Go and pick your losers at Wetherby, and when I'm through talking to Mr Upley, I'll come and have a word."

Rita laughed. "Losers at Wetherby? What day is this according to your calendar? He's picking losers at Plumpton."

Kepler put on another lascivious grin. "And for what I've got in mind, you won't need words." With a final cackle, he shuffled off to the reading room.

Upley's eyes followed them and I could almost see the line of daggers striking their way towards Kepler's back. "Picking his horses running at

Plumpton is, unfortunately, considered a legitimate use of the library's resources, but I can't help feeling that it would be better if I were permitted to test him and his ilk on their morning's reading."

That grumbling announcement persuaded me that Upley had missed his vocation. He should have been a teacher.

In order to distract him from the unscratchable irritation that was Harry Kepler, I brought our discussion full circle, and asked, "What is it you want me to do, precisely, Alden?"

"I thought I'd made that clear, Mrs Capper. We want you to pinpoint the thief. You do not have to confront him. Just tell us who it is, and at that point we will take over."

It was a tempting proposition, but as we continued negotiating, I tried to work out how to go about it. "Have you been authorised to meet my charges?"

For the first time, he was hesitant, vague. "Naturally, your bill will be paid from the council's treasury, which invariably entails some delay between presenting the invoice and final settlement."

"But they have agreed to meet the bill?"

"I, er... The details of the agreement are confidential, between myself, as head librarian, and the financial management team at the town hall. Can you give me an indication of the size of your bill?"

"Impossible. I don't know how long the job will take. I can tell you that I charge twenty pounds an hour, plus any out-of-pocket expenses, parking charges, petrol, wear and tear on equipment, and the like. If you think twenty pounds an hour is expensive, by all means shop around for other investigators. You'll find that they charge anything up to a hundred pounds an hour."

Upley chewed his lip. "If the task were to take you, let's say, fifty or sixty hours, then we'd be looking at a bill of well over a thousand pounds. That would be—"

I cut him off before he could sink into a quagmire at the bottom of which was potential bankruptcy for Haxford Borough Council. "For what I have in mind, Alden, it's unlikely to take that long, but before I can get into details on my methods, I'll need a lot more information." I spread my hands, gesturing around the library. "How many full shelves do you have? How many books are stored in this building? How many people come and go every day? Which of them is likely to have a book stuffed up his jumper? You see? It's the kind of crime that is difficult to narrow down, and that means my initial investigation must be tailored for any and every eventuality."

A tiny light showed in his dark blue eyes. "Well, as it happens, we can narrow the field down. You see…"

He trailed off as Patience Shuttle entered the building, and made her slow way to the counter.

Upley was full of unction once more. "Good morning, Miss Shuttle. I trust you are well."

His greasing grated on my sensibilities, but not as much as Patience's response. "We soldier on, Alden, soldier on."

According to my memory, Patience and her sisters, a pair of identical twins named Faith and Charity, were all in their eighties, part of one of those old families tied to Haxford for generations. Not that there was anything grand about them. You looked at their history and learned that their forefathers and foremothers were mill hands. That was back in the days when the town of Haxford processed wool. During my time on the beat, on those occasions when I had to call on them as a police officer, I found them sickly sweet, but masking a level of intolerance which demanded capital punishment for those hooligans who dared to dispose of empty crisp packets, sweet wrappers, and used condoms in their front garden. I always came away with the feeling that not one of the three sisters had ever used a condom for its designated purpose, but putting aside such prurient thoughts, what really used to rattle me was their sweetly-phrased complaints against the police. 'After all, dear, we do pay our taxes.' According to my estimate, they didn't work and therefore didn't pay a penny in tax. At one time, they relied upon their brother Robert for their income, but he disappeared some years ago, and how they managed now, I shuddered to think.

It was a curious thing, though. With the twins named Faith and Charity, you'd expect Patience to be named Hope, but then she was older than her sisters. She came along first, and I suppose their parents hadn't decided on the charm of a familiar trilogy of names.

Digging into a large shopping bag for the

book(s) she was returning, Patience bestowed a toothless smile upon me. "Good morning, Christine. Are you employed at the library now?"

"I'm afraid not, Patience. I'm here on business."

"A takeover bid? Well, I hope you'll keep Alden as head librarian."

I couldn't be bothered to correct her. "It would never occur to me to sack him."

Placing the books on the counter, Patience was not yet finished with me. "Have your son and his colleagues made any progress looking for the Graveyard Poisoner?"

"I have no idea," I replied. "I'm no longer with the police, and Simon tells me very little."

At that moment, Kim returned to deal with Patience, and Upley allowed her to take over, while he escorted me from behind the counter, and around the library until we reached the non-fiction section, where he gestured at a particular row of shelves.

"To continue our discussion, Mrs Capper, the books which have gone missing, about fifteen or twenty over the last year or two, are all from this section."

I checked the small, printed label on the edge of the shelf, and read, 'Medical/Biochemistry'. "Someone training to be a medical scientist?" I suggested.

"That is what we would like you to find out. I have a full list of the missing titles, and at an average of twenty-five pounds per book, we're talking a considerable sum of money."

I thought about Dennis's car and the many hundreds of pounds it cost to rebuild, and yet here was Upley, representing Haxford Borough Council, complaining about a loss of less than £500. If I spent more than twenty-five hours on the investigation, my bill would be higher than the amount they'd lost.

Still, mine was not to reason why. Mine was simply to further my reputation as a private investigator, and with the area of theft narrowed down so tightly, the investigative process suggested itself. Upley was right. There would be no need for confrontation.

I looked around. Although many of the bookshelves were lined along the wall, some were freestanding at right angles to said wall, and there was one such example eight feet from, parallel to and opposite the Medical/Biochemistry section. I looked further around. Aside from Patience Shuttle, now hobbling her way round Historical Romance, there were several other customers scanning the various shelves, some within earshot.

"We need to speak in private, Alden. Can we use the staff room?"

He agreed and we made our way to the back room where he switched on the kettle and prepared three beakers.

"I need some information," I said. "First, when did the last of these volumes disappear?"

He thought about it while preparing tea for us and Kim. By the time he placed a beaker in front of me, took one through to the counter, and then returned, he had the answer. "About five months ago."

"Do you have precise dates for when the other

volumes went missing?"

"No. It was only when we were subject to a complete audit that the missing volumes became apparent. Naturally, we've had several such audits in the past, and it was when the final numbers were compared that we realised just how many volumes had gone missing over the last couple of years. It was brought to my attention, and I was ordered to do something about it. Ms Aspinall suggested calling you. I rang the town hall and they said, 'go ahead', and here we are."

It occurred to me that it was entirely typical of Haxford Borough Council to learn of the missing books during the summer, and decide to do something about it in the run-up to Christmas.

"All right, here's what I want to do. I want to install a tiny camera on the general science shelf opposite the Medical/Biochemistry section. It's a wireless camera, and I should be able to pick it up on my laptop from here. If not, then I'll have to park at the back of the library on a day-to-day basis and monitor the feed until something occurs. That will cost you twenty pounds an hour, give or take, £140 a day."

Lines of worry creased his malleable features, and I jumped to an obvious conclusion.

"Alternatively, I can set the camera to store the video or even download to your system here in the library, and call in once-a-day to download the video feed. That would reduce your bill considerably."

My assumption that he was worrying about the cost was wrong. "Surveillance of that nature, Mrs

Capper, is illegal, isn't it?"

"So is stealing library books."

"Yes, but you don't fight crime—"

I was compelled to cut him off again. "Do you have security cameras in the library, Alden?"

"Well, yes, of course we do but—"

The accurately-timed Capper interrupt struck a second time. "There you are then. You don't tell them how many cameras you have, do you?"

"No, but they are quite large and attached to the walls. Anyone can see them."

"Mine will be tiny and unobtrusive, but it will still be visible. It's just that most people won't recognise it as a camera. Now what about it, Alden? Do we have agreement or do I come to the library every day and sit here for seven hours, nine until four… at twenty pounds an hour?"

"If you put it like that, fine." Upley offered his hand and we shook on the deal.

Chapter Four

It was almost half past ten when I left the library, stepping out into the icy cold of the day. The first snowflakes were in the air, tiny, white specs, swirling, whirling, looping the loop in a display of meteorological aerobatics before deciding on the precise spot where they would touch down, and then disappearing forever, thawed by the miniscule temperature differential between the air and the concrete or tarmac of the ground. A glance up at a sky the colour of the old lead pipes in the cellar of my parents' terraced house told me that before long it would come down heavier and it would 'stick' as settling was known in Haxford.

After reaching agreement with Upley I managed to get a word with Harry Kepler, but I had to wait while he and Rita were through nattering to Patience Shuttle. What they all had to talk about, I do not know. Probably the old days when Patience and Kepler's mother worked together in the mill. Possibly Rita's mother too. Whatever it was they were yattering for long enough, and they deployed similar small talk attempts with me, but a text from Dennis telling me my car was parked behind the library and did I have my keys, prompted me to a) reply to Dennis, *yes, and shouldn't you have asked me about the keys first thing*, and b) insist that Kepler get to the point: what had he seen or what did he know about the incident at Benny's.

"We saw Grimy on his way to t'dentist and he told me it was the Graveyard Poisoner. He was buying that weedkiller, parasquat from Benny who challenged him, so he shot old Benny and legged it."

Rita nodded. "It's true."

A further text from Dennis read, *why would I think to ask you. Your the clever one in this famly, not me.*

From the content, which irritated me, his misspelling of 'you're' and 'family' told me he had deliberately not used the predictive text facility of his phone and he did it to annoy me. He knew how to use it. Whatever else he might be, Dennis was not a technophobe. He used his laptop all the time when ordering spares or commenting on classic car forums.

I concentrated on the barflies. "The sale of Paraquat has been illegal since two thousand and seven," I told them, correcting Kepler's mispronunciation of the pesticide in question. "Lester Grimes is pulling your leg."

Rita disagreed. "No, no. He told me he got it from your Si."

And with that, I knew it was nonsense. With a stern reminder that I christened my son Simon, not Si, I left them studying the form for Plumpton.

And now I was outside watching the police dismantle their barriers to open the High Street again. I was tempted to take a walk along there, but time was getting on so I made my way to the small car park at the rear of the library and my little Renault Clio.

Tony Wharrier had done a smashing job on the paintwork. I don't know what shade the new wing was when it came from the main dealer, but Tony matched it perfectly with the older panels, and applied a coat of polish that made the car look spanking new.

As I settled into the driver's seat, I make a mental list of the things I needed to do before close of play that afternoon.

First, I needed to call home and pick up my little spy camera so I could place it in the library. If the book thief should strike that very day, I'd have him. After that, I needed to speak to Lester Grimes. A call to Dennis confirmed that Lester still hadn't arrived at the workshop, so I made for home where I picked up my spy camera, and then scooted back down to the library to get it in place.

This little bit of wi-fi magic cost me fifty pounds on the internet and it consisted of a tiny cube, not much bigger than a lump of sugar. It would run and record for about ninety minutes on battery, but while charging on the mains, it would run forever, and its SD card (which cost me extra) was good for sixteen gigabytes. I'd had it for about a year and I've been pining for an excuse to use it. So far, all I'd ever done with it was monitor the cat's antics when Dennis and I were both out working, and Cappy the Cat, our black and white, piebald moggie, was every bit as boring and lazy as Dennis with one major difference. At a pinch, I could get

Dennis to shift his backside and give me a hand round the house. Nothing short of the rattle of his feeding dish or the boom of a firework outside would shift Cappy the Cat. I often say how well-named he was. Cappy, was Dennis's nickname, as he pointed out earlier, and we christened the cat accordingly, adding 'the Cat' to differentiate between the two. And when it came to the fine art of doing sweet FA, they were in a class of their own.

Anticipating some wonderful images from the library, I positioned the camera on top of the shelves opposite Medical/Biochemistry, ran the cable along the top and borrowed some Sellotape to fasten it into place, then plugged it into a convenient wall socket, before picking it up on my laptop and checking the images, just to make sure it was aimed in the right direction. Satisfied, I then took a list of the stolen titles from Upley, before coming out of the library for the second time, and sat in my car deciding what to do next.

Even with a list of the stolen books, there was nothing I could do about them until I had some video to work on, so it was time to speak to Lester. The threatened snow hadn't yet begun to fall properly and as I drove south and west out of town, towards Haxford Mill, it needed only the occasional swish of the wipers to clear the little blobs off the windscreen.

Haxford is part of the old Heavy Woollen District and the Barncroft's Mill was built in the heady days of the Industrial Revolution, when it employed most of the town's working people.

Bequeathed to Haxford by the Barncroft family, the factory had long ago ceased to process wool and was now broken down into small units, evenly spread amongst its three floors, housing all sorts of cottage and not so cottage industries. Haxford Fixers was easily identified by the dirty signs above the place and the company van and wrecker outside the main door. Dennis and his partners rented two large units on the ground floor along the canal side of the mill. Those premises were expensive but necessary given the number of vehicles, motor cycles, lawnmowers, washing machines, tumble dryers, and other such domestic appliances they serviced, repaired, and often sold.

Dennis and Tony Wharrier used to work for Addison's, the largest car dealer and repair shop in Haxford, and both men had been there a long time. When it went under, they picked up a sizeable severance package. Three months later Haxford Fixers was born. I argued about the name, saying it made them sound like a branch of the local Mafia, but they were insistent, and from day one, they were inundated with work. But it wasn't just cars. A lot of people needed repairs to domestic appliances, and before long, Lester Grimes joined them, having been made redundant from the electrical contractors he worked for. The business was profitable and they were always busy, so much so that Dennis, as the auto specialist, often worked six full days a week.

Two cars – presumably waiting for attention or collection – stood outside the open doors of the workshop, and when I walked in, I found it in its usual state. Dennis was bent under the hood and working on the engine of a late-model, compact Kia, while behind him and across the workshop, a washing machine sat on a bench, its electrical innards exposed. Nearby was the door to the paint shop, this side of which Tony Wharrier, the hood of his overalls thrown back, his goggles raised to his forehead was poking the nozzle of a paint sprayer with a single bristle extracted from a wire brush, and as he did so, he was complaining.

"Ivy Saperia should make her mind up what colour she wants these kitchen doors. First it was magnolia, then it was brilliant white, and now it's fiery – whatever that's supposed to mean... oh. Hello, Christine. I didn't see you there."

"Good afternoon, Tony. You can take it from me that Ivy Saperia wouldn't know the difference between magnolia and custard, and if she said fiery, she probably meant ivory."

Dennis straightened up, knocked his head on the raised bonnet of the Kia and backed out from under it. "Hey up, Chrissy, what are you doing here? Nowt wrong with the car is there?"

"The car's fine, Dennis." I beamed a smile on Tony. "And thanks for doing such a good job on the paint, spit and polish."

"My pleasure." He glanced at Dennis. "As long as your old man settles the bill sharpish."

"You'll get your money." Dennis turned back to me. "So if the car's all right, what do you want?"

"Lester. I want a few words with him."

Dennis tutted and ducked back under the car bonnet, leaving any further debate to Tony who told me, "He rang in this morning with toothache. Said he was going to the dentist. Then he got bogged down with that business on the High Street, turned up here about half an hour ago, and now he's gone up to Sandra's Snacky. I mean, should he be eating while his mouth is still numb?"

"His trap might be numb, but it didn't stop him from yapping," Dennis declared from under the Kia's hood.

Ignoring my husband, I said, "He might slobber a little, but it shouldn't stop him from eating."

"If he is slobbering, no one will notice the difference," Tony said.

I had no more interest in Lester Grimes's dental problems than I had in Ivy Saperia's kitchen, so I changed the subject. "I need to speak to him. He was a witness to the incident this morning."

Dennis tutted once more, this time from under the Kia's hood. "Poking your nose in again?"

Tony refrained from responding to my husband's allegation, and shifted the discussion sideways once more. "Well, if you're going upstairs to see him, could you tell him that Jammy has been in this morning nagging over that washing machine?" Tony pointed to the offending item sitting on the bench.

"Jammy?"

"Jamal Patel," Dennis translated, coming out from under the hood again and selecting a different spanner. "Grimy promised Jammy that washer would be ready last Friday, and that's as far as it's got. And he's in a bit of a snit... Jammy, not Grimy. He's got a bloke coming round to look at it sometime today, and according to Jammy, if the buys he wants it installed before Christmas."

"A job for you boys?" I asked. "You can install it on Jamal's behalf, can't you?"

"No sweat," Tony said with an air of hubris. "But it would have to be Cappy or me. I wouldn't trust Lester Grimes to install new coasters on our coffee table. Not if he's been in the Sump Hole the night before."

"I'll try to persuade him."

***

Dennis and his partners made no excuses for being regulars at Sandra's Snacky on the third floor of the mill. The prices were cheap-ish, preparation and presentation near perfect, and if Sandra's surname, Limpkin, made her the butt of many derogatory jokes, she was one of those tough, old school Haxforders who could take the flak and return it.

The latter was familiar territory to me. I put up with more than my share of theoretical humour when I ceased to be Christine Fordice and took Dennis's surname. Capper the Copper was the favourite when I was a police officer, as evidenced by Harry Kepler earlier. It's all part of life in Haxford, and even I tolerated it until it became tiresome, whereupon I resorted to matronly disapproval and lessons in simple politeness.

The Snacky was in the thickest throes of lunchtime demands when I got there, and Sandra and her two assistants flitted around like flies homing in on a compost heap. It was some time before I got to order a cheese salad sandwich and a cup of tea.

"It ain't often we see you here, Chrissy," Sandra said, pouring the tea. "Missing Dennis, were you? Bought him summat special for Christmas? Frilly underwear and a promise maybe?"

I smiled. "If I bought frilly underwear, he'd take it to work and use it to wipe the oil off his hands while he was servicing someone's car."

Sandra slid the tea and sandwich across the counter, took my money and dropped it in the till. "Must be handy though. You know. When summat goes wrong with your car."

"He's probably saved us hundreds over the years, so I mustn't moan, but..." I took my change. "Anyway, it's not him I've come to see. It's Lester Grimes." I nodded across the partitioned area harbouring the Snacky's crowded tables to where Lester sat alone in the doldrums..

"Grimy? He's in a right mood today. Toothache or something. Good luck with him is all I can say."

Lester was a year older than Dennis but he looked five or ten years older. He was a rarity in Haxford inasmuch as he'd been married and divorced twice. Marriage was becoming rarer, and although the town had its share of deserted wives (and husbands, I should imagine) divorce was almost unheard of, but Lester had achieved it twice, and on both occasions it was the same problem: his fondness for Haxford Best Bitter.

Not that he was alcoholic, but simply that he liked to call for a couple of pints on the way home from work every night, and over the weekend, that 'couple of pints' usually turned into a full blown, evening session, often in The Engine House pub where he enjoyed his turn on the karaoke.

I'd heard him sing on a number of occasions and he has an excellent, tenor voice, but it seemed at odds alongside the rest of him. Short, wrinkled, similar to Harry Kepler, he shaved perhaps once a week and only then when the whiskers began to irritate him, and he washed when he felt like it, which according to Dennis was never more than twice a week. And it wasn't only in appearance that he resembled Harry Kepler. He had the same devil-may-care approach, especially where women were concerned, something which I put down to the beer, and he had been heard to say that he couldn't understand how he's never been beaten to a pulp by some jealous husband. I long ago learned to ignore his suggestive leer and innuendo.

"Hello, Lester. You're looking a little sorry for yourself."

"Toothache, Chrissy. Driving me mad, it is." He reached across the table and took my hand. "I could do with soft, female fingers to soothe me fettered brow. I reckon Dennis wouldn't mind."

"Dennis probably wouldn't notice, but I would." I retracted my hand and started work on my sandwich. "Tony asked me to tell you that Jamal Patel is on the warpath. Something about a washing machine."

"Gar. Flaming foreigners."

I swallowed the bite of cheese, lettuce and tomato, and helped it down with a sip of tea. "His parents or grandparents might have come from… wherever, but Jamal was born here in this country. He's not a foreigner."

"Yes he is. He comes from Accrington, and that's Lancashire." Lester took a mouthful of tea and winced as his toothache bit him. "Could be worse, I suppose. He coulda been a Geordie."

"Lester—"

"Never understand a word they say, Geordies."

Everyone is welcome in Yorkshire, I thought to myself, but for preference, they should be born under the white rose.

Lester's attitude was partly the child of his upbringing, but mostly a half-hearted attempt at humour. He was no more racist, anti-Lancastrian or anti-Tyneside than me. His first wife was a Manchester woman, and his second wife came from Middlesbrough, and in both cases, he met them when he was working on building sites in their locale.

He was an electrician by trade, and as a partner in Haxford Fixers, he handled all electrical work, which in this day and age also meant electronics in the shape of wiring and control units in vehicles, automatic washing machines and the like, but he steered clear of computer and entertainment equipment such as televisions, CD and DVD players, and as he freely admitted, he was too old for climbing ladders to realign aerials or install satellite equipment.

"So what you doing here, Chrissy? I thought Dennis took your car back to you."

"He did. I'm here to see you, Lester."

His unshaven features lit up. "It's my lucky day."

"I had enough of that from Harry Kepler. I want

to know what happened with Benny Barnes. Kim says she saw you on the High Street this morning."

"Ah. The brouhaha at Benny's Bargain Basement." He grinned showing few teeth, all of them nicotine stained. "I made that up meself, you know. Not bad is it? The brouhaha at Benny's Bargain Basement."

"It's very clever. You obviously missed your vocation somewhere along the line. But what actually happened at Benny's?"

Lester screwed up his face, and closed his eyes as if either trying to fight off his toothache or jog his memory. "Well, y'see, I wasn't actually inside the shop. I was just walking past, on me way to the dentist. This'd be about quarter past eight. I had to be at the dentist for nine and you know me. I don't drive no more, so I had to get the bus to town. And the buses only run when they feel like it, so I was well early. And have you seen the price they charge on the buses?"

Lester lost his licence after being breathalysed a few years previously and he made the decision to give up driving altogether. It was either that or give up the beer.

"Let's not get sidetracked. What happened at Benny's?"

"Still a copper at heart, aren't you, Chrissy? Can't let it rest, can you?"

"It's news, Lester, and I like to put news on my vlog, which is a video blog, as you would know if you ever went online."

"The nearest I get to online is hanging me shorts out on a washing line. Aye, and I don't do that so often. Not at this time of year."

"Benny's," I prompted him.

"Well, as I say, I were only walking past when I heard these two shots and Benny shouting out. Then two young'uns came running out and legged it down the road. Mind, they weren't carrying guns, so I ran into the paper shop next door, just to get out of the way, and I rang the plod from there."

I tried to hide my surprise. "You didn't go in to see how Benny was?"

"What? And find the shooter still hanging about in there? Not likely. I've seen enough Clint Eastwood fillums to know to keep me nose out. As I say, those kids legged it sharp enough, and they weren't carrying no gun or I'd have seen it. No, whoever did it was still inside."

"All right. So what happened next?"

"About twenty minutes later, your Simon turned up and so did half the police station. I had to wait ages for 'em to take a statement from me. I were late for the dentists and I had to wait again there. That's why Jammy's washer isn't finished."

"I'm not really interested in Jamal's washing machine. What about Benny? Did you learn anything?"

"Nobody was saying nowt, not even your Simon, but they carted him off to t'ozzy in an ambulance. Benny, not your Simon."

"The hospital?" I took in another mouthful of tea. "Not the mortuary?"

"I don't think so. It were an ordinary ambulance, and them mortuary ambulances is usually black, aren't they?" Lester finished his tea and stood up.

"I'll have to get back, Chrissy. I need a smoke first, and if I don't get a move on with that washer, Jammy won't pay me, and it's karaoke tomorrow night at the Sump Hole. I'll catch you later, luv."

He left and I sipped at my tea. Too much of what Lester told me was assumption. He hadn't witnessed anything other than two young men running away and an ambulance carrying Benny Barnes off to hospital. There was little point talking to Simon yet. Even if he knew anything he still wouldn't tell me. Better to wait until he finished his shift then play him along as only a mother could.

In the meantime, I decided I'd be better visiting the hospital to see what Benny himself had to say… if he was in a position to say anything.

Chapter Five

Haxford never aspired to anything grander than a cottage hospital. Most health issues were handled at GP level, while accidents and other, slightly more urgent medical requirements were taken or sent to Haxford Cottage Hospital – known locally as The Cottage. Major accidents and emergencies were the province of Huddersfield, ten miles away and complex surgery usually meant a trip to Leeds, Bradford or Wakefield.

Coming out of Haxford Mill at a quarter to two, just as the first proper snowflakes were beginning to fall, I realised I had no idea where the ambulance might have taken Benny. A quick call to Simon put the matter right but only after some negotiation.

"I told you I can't tell you anything, Mam."

"I'm not asking you to tell me what happened, Simon. I just want to know where Benny is. I want to reassure my followers that he's all right."

Simon tutted. "You'll get me hung one of these days. They took him to The Cottage. Whether he's still there or whether they shifted him to Huddersfield, I can't say, but Barry was with him."

Barry Barnes was Benny's twenty-four-year-old son.

"Thank you. Don't forget Christmas lunch on

Saturday."

"The number of times you keep reminding me, I'm not likely to forget, am I?"

"That's what mothers are there for. Give my love to Bethany and tell her Santa will be calling at our house on Friday night as well as yours."

"Yes, Mother."

It was always a sure sign that, just as when Dennis called me Christine instead of Chrissy, Simon's use of 'mother' instead of 'mam', meant he was beginning to lose patience, so I rang off and drove out of the mill for the two-mile trip to The Cottage.

Imagine Haxford as a clock face – which served to remind me that my clock was still in need of Christmas glad rags when I could find the time to pick them up – the mill was located at about four o'clock and The Cottage at eleven o'clock, which meant I had to drive through the town again, and while not as bad as first thing, the by-pass was heaving with traffic. It was especially bad at the entrance to the CutCost supermarket, the largest in town, and it further reminded me that aside from the Christmas extras, I still had my essential shopping to do for the extended weekend holiday. The shops would be closed for anything up to four days, and with Dennis at home more than usual, Simon, Naomi, and Bethany calling at regular intervals, and maybe even Ingrid and her boyfriend paying a flying visit, I daren't be without bread, milk, eggs, butter, cat food and washing up liquid; the staple necessities of life.

Dennis, I decided, would come with me when he

finished work on Thursday, the day before Christmas Eve. He would no doubt complain, but then, that's what husbands are good at, especially when they have to cover the bill at the checkout.

The Cottage stood just off Huddersfield Road, in its own, pleasant grounds at the upper end of Barncroft Memorial Park. A large, Victorian building, more in keeping with a manor house than a hospital, its stone was blackened with age, and it gave out a slightly forbidding air, but inside it was as modern and well-equipped as any small hospital. There were a few, short-stay wards, but with the exception of maternity, most of its routine, day-to-day work was of the patch 'em up and send 'em home variety.

When I walked in, I found the large waiting area as busy as ever with patients, many of whom, I guessed, were here for minor trauma, the kind of slips and bumps, knocks and falls which went hand in hand with a Yorkshire winter.

I didn't know the prim and proper reception clerk, but she knew me – probably a vlog viewer – and she refused point bank to divulge any information regarding Benny Barnes. "I'm sorry, Mrs Capper, but there is such a thing as patient confidentiality, you know. I can't tell you anything about Mr Barnes."

"I'm a friend of Benny's… well, one of his most faithful customers—"

"So are most of Haxford, but you're also a reporter, and even ignoring that, it makes no difference. I'm not allowed to discuss patients other than with their families."

I let out a huffy sigh. It caused me to wonder how real reporters coped with this kind of obduracy. I was tempted to launch a rant on my vlog, but I dismissed the idea the moment it occurred to me. Vitriol was not my forte.

"I'm a commentator, not a reporter, and I'm only asking if he's still here."

"And I can't tell you."

"But I can." I turned to find Detective Sergeant Amanda Hiscoe behind me. "Hi, Chrissy. I saw you there and I guessed you were chasing up the Benny Barnes story."

Somewhere the right side of forty, Amanda was the senior CID officer in Haxford and had been for a number of years. She came under the watchful eye of Detective Inspector Patrick Quinn, who moved to Huddersfield after his last promotion. Mandy, as she preferred to be addressed, was a vivacious blonde, unmarried by choice, and a solid, hard-working detective, with a fine record. In my opinion, she'd make a good inspector, but she was Haxford born and bred and had no desire to move from her hometown, and naturally, the low-level crimes prevalent in Haxford did not warrant a detective inspector on permanent station. It's how come we got rid of Paddy Quinn.

"Good to see you, Mandy. Are you looking forward to having Simon working with you in the New Year?"

"He has a lot to learn. I know. I've been there, but if he's anything like his mum he'll pick it up quickly. Come on. Let's let tight-lips hug her secrets and grab a cup of coffee while I clue you up."

The Cottage did not run to a cafeteria, only vending machines, and at length, we took our coffee out into the cold afternoon, and sat in Mandy's car where she ran the heaters. Handy having a mileage account. That way the police would pay for your petrol, even when you're only running the engine to keep warm.

I fired the opening shots. "I asked Simon what happened and he said he can't tell me anything."

Mandy chuckled. "It's all about Paddy Quinn going over the top. When doesn't he? When Grimy rang in reporting gunshots, it all hit the fan, and Paddy came zipping down from Huddersfield like he was leading the flying squad, and he put an immediate ban on us talking to the press, public, whoever."

"Yet you're talking to me."

"He overreacted, Chrissy. You know what he's like."

And I did know him. I worked with Quinn when he was a uniformed constable and I was a probationer fresh out of training, and he always gave out the air of an overworked, underpaid permanently harassed police officer. There's nothing wrong with the principle. The police were always stretched, and while the pay had improved over the years, I nevertheless knew of lorry drivers who were earning more. In Quinn's case, however, he always went about his business wearing a frown and with a snap in his voice, an image he'd almost certainly developed from old TV shows like The Sweeney, and when something cropped up, it was all hands to the pumps, with squad cars flying through the streets like they were policing the track at Brands Hatch.

I brought my mind back to the here and now. "So what happened?"

"Truth is, we don't know. Grimy rang in reporting gunshots. At Benny's? It didn't seem likely, but we had other witnesses who heard it and who saw two young kids, teenagers, running hell for leather out of the shop and away along the High Street. That was just after quarter past eight. Course, when Paddy got the news, his head was full of armed blaggers... in Benny's? I sometimes wonder if Paddy thinks he's working in New York. Anyway, he put an embargo on anyone speaking to anyone. I'm surprise he didn't call for an armed response unit. He also ordered the High Street shut, and you know what kind of a mess that caused."

I sampled a wet of insipid coffee and scowled, but my grimace was not caused by the coffee alone. "My car was off the road until mid-morning, and Dennis had to take me to town. We got caught up in it."

"I told you. A bog standard, Paddy Quinn overreaction," Mandy repeated. "By the time Paddy got there from Huddersfield, I'd already been into the shop and the only person there was Benny... spark out on the floor."

"That was extraordinarily brave of you, Mandy."

The detective shook her head and her shower of blonde curls wafted from side to side. "Not really. We'd been there twenty minutes and we hadn't seen or heard anything. Someone had to go in and check it out. I figured if there really was a gunman, he'd take me hostage, and I was prepared to settle for that. As it happens, there was no one. The back door was open, so whoever was in there probably legged it that way. I tell you, there was not a soul. Aside from Benny, that is. And he was out for the count." She shuddered at the memory, flipped the lid of her coffee and took a swig. "At first I thought he was dead. He wasn't moving at all, but I checked his pulse and he was still alive. I belled the ambulance. Paddy threw a fit when he found out what I'd done, and we had a bit of a ding-dong in his car." Now she laughed. "The day hasn't dawned when I can't deal with Paddy Quinn. I told him, I said, my first thought was for Benny. He wasn't moving and I couldn't bring him round. He needed medical attention. Anyway, the paramedics turned up, checked him over and said there was a nasty bump and a cut at the back of his head, and he was still unresponsive. They brought him here and the trauma people said it was beyond their brief or their capability, so they shuffled him off to Huddersfield Royal. Last update I got was by phone about an hour ago and he still hasn't come round." The frown returned to her clear brow. "I was worried, Chrissy. I mean, Benny is an institution in this town, isn't he?"

"Not so much Benny as the Barneses as a family," I agreed. "We've all grown up with the bargain shop, haven't we? When I was a young copper like you, his dad ran the place and it was Billy's Best Buys. Benny used to help his dad in the same way that Barry helps Benny, and I suppose when Benny retires. Barry will take the place over."

Mandy smiled without a trace of humour. "When we were kids, we used to go in and nick sweets off the counter. One of us would distract Billy or Benny by making a mess of the cheap toys, and while he wasn't looking, we'd be filling our pockets." Her smile faded again. "And he's not old, is he? Benny, I mean, not Billy."

"Billy passed away a couple of years ago, and Benny is about my age, I think. I know Barry's a bit younger than our Simon." I shifted the topic sideways. "So if Benny has been moved to Huddersfield, what are you doing here?" I gestured up at The Cottage.

"Personal."

"Oh. Nothing serious, I hope."

"Depends how you define serious. I took something I shouldn't have."

My mind automatically focused on illegal drugs, yet I never thought Mandy was the type. "Took something? Like what?" I asked.

"Like a man." She sighed again. "Great romp at the time, but I'm not sure I want a child in my life just yet."

Romp? Irresponsible was my opinion. What was I saying about the Shuttle sisters and condoms? I kept my thoughts to myself and asked, "Confirmed or a false alarm?"

Her face sagged. "Positive. I need to think what to do about it, Chrissy."

It was not something I wanted to discuss, but the life of a single mother, a Haxford police officer to boot, might make an acceptable topic for the vlog sometime in the future. It was never an issue for me. I joined the police at age twenty, and resigned seven or eight years later when I fell pregnant with Simon. As I said earlier, the risks to police officers tended to be overstated in the tabloid press, but they were there and neither I nor Dennis wanted Simon and Ingrid to be left without a mother while they were still children.

I brought us back on topic. "All right. Have you spoken to Barry?"

Mandy nodded. "He was late for work – thanks to Paddy Quinn's hastiness in closing the High Street. By the time he came walking down the street all hell was breaking loose. He doesn't know what happened and when we'd done with him, he followed the ambulance here and I assume he's shot off to Huddersfield with his dad."

"I'll give him a ring later, find out how Benny's getting on." I swallowed another mouthful of the coffee. "Dear me, this is awful. The coffee, I mean. Mind you, what's happened is just as bad. You'll be looking for the two youngsters who ran away, will you?"

"Definitely. No one recognised them... or, let's say that no one's owned up to recognising them. You could do us a favour, Chrissy. We got some footage from a few High Street cameras. Would you mind coming to the station and looking at them, see if you can make these two toe rags out? I'll not tell you who I think they were – well, one of them anyway. I'd be interested in your unbiased opinion."

It was an invitation I'd been hoping for, and if

Mandy had not asked, I would have suggested it. "Only too pleased to help. Are you on your way back there now?"

Mandy held up her wax cup. "The minute I've finished this rubbish coffee."

I returned to my car and when Mandy pulled away, I fell in behind her.

The police station was off the northern bypass. Built in the early 1970s, it was new in comparison to the buildings surrounding it, most of which were pre-war, and in some cases, pre-Boer-War. Along with most of the town's police force, I was stationed there, and these days, the men and women able to recall working out of the old, Victorian base on Wakefield Street (now a carpet showroom) were retired or on the verge of handing in their warrant card and cashing in on their pension.

Most of the Haxford police knew me, if not personally, then through my vlog or my work as a private investigator, and as I accompanied Mandy to the main office, where a crowd of officers, some in uniform, others in civilian clothes were working at one task or another, quite a few of them greeted me with a cheery 'hello', a wave, or a smile.

That did not apply to my son, who groaned when he laid eyes on me in the corridor. "Mother. I thought I told you—"

"Oh, do be quiet, Simon. Mandy invited me. Remember what I always told you about which orders to disobey? Well, Mandy learned that lesson."

He looked to his sergeant who grinned back at him. "Stop fretting, Simon. You'll learn."

I followed Mandy to her small enclave in the far corner of the room, where, partitioned off from prying eyes, she ran the security camera footage for me. It came from one traffic camera and footage from two other institutions.

Without the consent of individuals captured on video, audio recording was illegal, and the major problem with this footage was the silence, making it impossible to hear the alleged gunshot from Benny's. Mandy, however, assured me that several people testified to it.

"We haven't uncovered any trace of a weapon having been used. No spent cartridges or shot, but the forensic boys haven't finished their work yet."

Of the video they had recovered, the camera at the traffic lights on the junction of Yorkshire Street gave the best view along the entire length of the High Street, and it was readily apparent when the gunshot occurred because so many heads turned in the direction of Benny's, including that of Lester Grimes, who, as he told me, was passing at that exact moment. The time signature on the recording indicated fourteen minutes past eight.

A second later, two slender young men came hurrying from the shop, and ran off away from the camera, towards the junction with Huddersfield Street. The distance from the camera made it almost impossible to discern any features, but I noticed a shock of unruly, red hair belonging to one.

"That looks like young John Frogshaw," I said.

Mandy agreed with a triumphant smile. "Exactly what I said. Course, we haven't been able to find him yet, and even when we do, he'll have half a dozen mates to swear he was in church for choir practice at the time."

Dark thoughts rushed round my head while I checked out the other footage. That taken from the bank adjacent to Benny's place was focussed on the ATM outside the bank, and useless. Lester Grimes was clearly visible as he walked past, but the field of view was narrowed to the adjacent pavement. All I could see of the pair running away was their feet, both wrapped in expensive looking trainers, but even then, it was only for a brief second. The same was true of the video coming from the camera outside the Haxford Building Society on the other side of the street which yielded a similarly narrow view.

I gave up. "I'm sorry, Mandy, but other than young Frogshaw, I can't help you."

With my wristwatch reading three o'clock, I left the police station and climbed into my car. The snow was coming down heavier now, not blizzardy but significant, beginning to settle, and I was thinking of calling it day, going home before Moor Road, the way up to Bracken Close, became too difficult to negotiate.

But I couldn't. Not while I needed to speak to Barry Barnes, not while I had a camera running at the library, and not while Lester Grimes had questions to answer.

Chapter Six

It was quarter past three when I pulled up outside Haxford Fixers for the second time in under three hours. The firm's van hadn't moved and neither had the wrecker. More significantly, neither had either of the two cars presumably waiting for my old man's attention. In common with his classic Morris Marina they sported a fine dusting of snow on the windscreens, but then, the Marina hadn't moved either.

Digging into the deeper recesses of my smartphone's directory, I eventually found Barry Barnes's mobile number and rang it. The conversation did not last long.

"I'm sorry, Christine, but I can't talk right now. I'm still at Huddersfield Royal. Mum's here, so's Vicky, my missus, and we're all too upset."

"Your father hasn't regained consciousness yet?"

"Not yet. It's very worrying."

"I can imagine. Well listen, Barry, give my regards to your mum and your wife, and I hope Benny recovers very soon. I'll ring again tomorrow to see if we can get together for five or ten minutes."

"I'll do that, and thanks, Christine."

All right, so I wasn't pushy enough to make a

true investigative reporter, but that did not mean to say I couldn't turn on the hard stuff when I had to… like right now with Lester Grimes.

When I walked into the workshop, Dennis was still working under the hood of the Kia. Tony Wharrier was conspicuous by his absence but I could hear him working away in the paint shop, and the only change from lunchtime was in Lester, whose head was inside the washing machine Jamal Patel was (allegedly) waiting for.

"Are you washing your hair, Lester?" I asked, causing Dennis to come out from under the Kia's raised bonnet, a stupid grin plastered across his face.

Lester said something but because he was still inside the washing machine, his words were unintelligible.

"He's in trouble," Dennis told me. "Jammy paid us a call not long after you left and he's steaming… which is more than the washing machine does."

"I don't care about Mr Patel's washing machine," I said. "I'm more interested in why Lester didn't tell me the truth earlier."

I couldn't hear Lester, but it was certain that he heard my last comment because it caused him to back out of the washing machine, stand up straight, turn and face me. "I told you everything, Chrissy. You're not a copper no more, so why are you poking your nose in?"

"I've just been speaking to Mandy Hiscoe, and she invited me to have a look at the video feed from cameras on the High Street this morning. I saw you, Lester, and I saw the two teenagers who were running away from Benny's after the… whatever the incident was. Why didn't you tell me that one of them was young Johnny Frogshaw?"

Dennis pulled the kind of face that he reserves for motorists when he has to deliver bad news about their vehicles. The kind of face that said, 'this is tough, and it's gonna cost you a fortune'.

Lester struggled to make eye contact. "Listen, Chrissy, nobody with any brains grasses up young Froggy. You start ratting on him and the next thing you know, his dad, Jacko, is paying you a visit, and when he comes a-calling, he's usually carrying a hammer. My knees might not be pretty, but I prefer them where they are and in one piece. Besides, I don't know for sure that it was young Froggy. I know the kid was a bloodnut, but to be honest, I was more concerned with getting into the paper shop and keeping out the way of the shooter, who I thought was still in Benny's."

I was aware of the Frogshaws' reputation, but I didn't think people like Lester Grimes would be intimidated, especially considering the way he often laid a line of suggestive chat on any number of married women, running the risk of a reaction from angry husbands.

"So, in reality, you're a simple coward."

Dennis decided it was time he contributed to the discussion, and disagreed with my analysis. "He's no chicken, lass. It's common sense. Start hassling with Froggy, senior or junior, and the next thing you know, your classic car is a classic bonfire… while you're still behind the wheel."

"I don't think that'll put Mandy Hiscoe or Paddy

Quinn off. But you don't have to grass them up, Lester. Just tell me. Was it Johnny Frogshaw running away from Benny's?"

Lester scratched the back of his neck, then the thin hair above his left ear, and rubbed his nose. "Well, see, Chrissy, like I said, I wasn't taking that much notice."

"But they weren't carrying guns. You said so earlier. What's that if it's not taking notice?"

"Yeah, but I was looking at their hands, not their faces. I meanersay, they wouldn't be carrying shotguns in their teeth, would they?"

I sigh. "It doesn't matter. I'll call out and speak to Frogshaw myself."

Concern spread quickly over my husband's face. "Hang about, Chrissy. I know you like poking your nose in, but do you have to be so stupid? It doesn't make any difference that you're a woman, you know. He'll still smash your face in."

I gave him my sweetest mock-smile. "You forget, Dennis, I'm not only a woman, but an ex-cop. You leave Jack Frogshaw to me."

I turned on my heels, marched out of the workshop, and climbed into my car. It was gone half past three, and early December darkness was descending on the town, the gloom exacerbated by light snow, now falling consistently.

Time was getting on once again, and after the brief, non-event conversation with Lester I still had two calls to deal with – in theory. Frogshaw's and the library. The library was the most pressing. The doors closed at half past four and Upley was never in favour of working overtime. I had to download the afternoon's footage onto my laptop and I could see that by the time I finished there, night would be with us, and I didn't fancy the drive out to the Frogshaws' place. They lived on an old farm up on the moors, a mile or two out of town, and with the weather closing in I guessed it would be better to leave it until the morning. After all, I wasn't contracted to learn what happened at Benny's Bargain Basement. It was a matter of interest, not an 'earner' as Dennis would describe it.

The decision taken, I made for town once again, and pulled into the car park behind the library at a few minutes to four. The journey which would normally take ten minutes took almost twenty; a sure sign that the weather and the pre-Christmas rush, combined with the school run and encroaching night was already taking its toll.

The library was not busy. No one in the reading room, one or two browsers scanning the shelves, Upley and Kim drifting into that thumb-twiddling wind-down before closing time.

Setting up my laptop in the staff room, I downloaded the afternoon's video footage, and was surprised to find that it took up seven of the sixteen available gigabytes. According to my calculations it would have to run for an additional two or three hours the following day, so just to be on the safe side, I would have to call to the library twice, download the footage at lunchtime, and then call again near to closing time to download a second lot. Never mind it would all go on the final bill.

The download was slow, too, and it took all of fifteen minutes before everything was secure on my laptop, and I could clear the camera memory. For once, Kim was an authority on the matter.

"It's not the connection, Chrissy, but your laptop. It's time you invested in a new one. Something with a faster chip."

The thought did not fill me with joy. "But I've only had this eight years."

Kim laughed. "Eight years? These things are usually obsolete in less than twelve months."

I began to pack away my equipment. "Whatever you do, don't tell Dennis that. You're probably too young to remember, but there was a time when obsolescence was built into motor cars, and it's only dinosaurs like Dennis, men – and women, too, I suppose – who are obsessed with rebuilding classic cars who won't have it. If he learns that obsolescence is built into computers, Ingrid will have nowhere to sleep when she visits because our spare bedrooms will be full of hard drives, motherboards, and other technological gubbins."

From the library it was a five-minute journey home, but it took almost fifteen, and I think I did rather well. The car only slid on the snow three or four times, and for once, instead of driving into the drive, I actually managed to reverse in without getting dangerously close to either gatepost.

Cappy the Cat was pleased to see me, but in an awful hurry to get out into the garden. He deployed a rapid change of plan when I opened the back door for him. He sniffed at the air, checked out the light, falling snow, and instead made for his litter tray. I swear Dennis was training that cat.

I had much to do but it was relegated to a back

seat when set alongside the need to feed Cappy the Cat and follow it with a cup of tea and a warm in front of the fire. I had the library footage to check and our evening meal to prepare and cook.

Many of my friends protested at the latter. Was there something wrong with Dennis taking his turns at cooking? After all, in this day and age of increasing emancipation, men should do their share in the kitchen. Perfectly true, but there was a snag, and it went by the name of Dennis. His cooking ability is limited to toast, and he could only get that right because the toaster had a timer. With anything else he was hopeless. Boiled eggs? The pan always boils over or the eggs crack when he drops them in, and I do mean drop. He could manage a pan of chips, but it would be taking a risk, as he pointed out the last time the chip pan caught fire. That cost us not only a spanking new deep fat fryer, but also a coat of paint on the ceiling, some hard scrubbing at the tiles behind the cooker, and fresh wallpaper behind and above the offending appliance. Where Dennis is concerned, grilling anything is as big a risk, usually because he gets distracted by phone calls, and he's never understood why you need to turn the bacon or sausages over.

"How come the grill doesn't do both sides at once?" he asked.

The difference between the grill facility of a standard cooker and the George Foreman grill is not something I could easily explain to Dennis, because he would want all the technical ins and outs, but the question did prompt him to consider designs for a two-sided grill as part and parcel of your average kitchen stove.

There was also the time factor to consider. Dennis rarely got home before seven in the evening, and if I had to wait for him doing the cooking, we would probably sit down to eat at half past eight. Since I rarely went out, except on those rare occasions when I was on a case, it was simpler for me to deal with it. At such times when I had to be out in the evening (again, it was not very often) I usually cooked his meal and left it in the microwave with instructions on how to warm it up. Yes, he did need instructions.

Finally, there was the decision to make. If I said to him "What do you fancy for tea?" (we common folk always called our evening meal, 'tea') he would invariably answer, "Summat with chips." Naturally, I ensured he ate a relatively balanced diet. He's a big man, tall, muscular. It comes from doing a fairly heavy job of work. If I gave way and rustled up fried food every day, he would be tall, muscular, and fat.

Tonight, however, he would get part of his way. I had too much to do without having to prepare a large meal, so he was granted a steak pie (from the freezer because I didn't have time to faff about with pastry, and anyway, we didn't have any fresh meat in) mashed potatoes, with a serving of processed peas, and he only got those because I had a can open.

With Cappy the Cat curled up on my lap and a warming cup of tea inside me, heat permeating the room from the fire and radiators, drowsiness threatened, but I was short of time. Aside from peeling potatoes, I had the library video to study and a glance at the clock revealed... that I still hadn't climbed the stepladder to drape some tinsel over it. I hadn't even bought the tinsel. The clock also told me it was getting on for half past five.

Ignoring his protest, I shuffled Cappy the Cat off my lap and into a corner of the settee, from where he glowered at me in the way only mean-spirited cats could, while I fired up the laptop, and with a fresh brew at my elbow, I opened the video.

Dennis had this thing about modern movies. He denounced most of them as 'tripe' but he didn't restrict his stark opinion exclusively to the modern stuff. He felt the same way about a fair proportion of the films which were aimed at 'our generation'. I recalled he was particularly scathing about the BBC adaptation of John le Carre's *Tinker, Tailor, Soldier, Spy*. He and I were burgeoning teenagers when it was first shown, but we recently caught a rerun, and notwithstanding a top notch cast he declared it as interesting as watching paint dry.

Fred Timmins, our next door neighbour, once set up a night camera hoping to catch hedgehogs in his back garden. This despite the fact that sightings of hedgehogs on Bracken Close are as frequent as sightings of Bengal tigers; in other words, never. Fred seemed to think that it would make a suitable vlog post and he showed me some of the video he had taken. It consisted of a static shot of his back garden with water and feeding bowls on the lawn, and that was it. The video ran for eight solid hours and the only thing of any interest was a sparrow homing in on the water at sunrise. Cappy the Cat didn't even put in an appearance, and he usually makes for the Timmins's garden when he needs to relieve himself. I swear Dennis has trained Cappy the Cat to do that. He doesn't like Fred Timmins. Dennis doesn't like him, I mean, not Cappy the Cat, although I suspect our cuddly moggie feels the same way on account of Barbara Timmins's habit of shooing him out of her garden.

All this ran through my mind as I watched the video from the library. I suddenly understood Dennis's reaction to *Tinker, Tailor* and why I rejected Fred Timmins's video out of hand. Boring doesn't come into it. This was tedium on an Olympic scale. After ten minutes, I set the video speed to x16 and it still took a further twenty minutes to get through it.

Throughout the four and half hours, less than a dozen people visited that section, and one of those was Kim who spent several minutes putting books back on the shelves. I recognised Rita Nuffield, but there was nothing to interest her. Patience Shuttle put in an appearance, but she was looking at the shelf under the camera, the general science section, and a little later Harry Kepler himself turned up and took down a book from the Medical/Biochemistry shelf. That was easy to explain. He couldn't hang around the pubs because he had no money and he needed an excuse to sit in the reading room. A textbook on Advanced Brain Surgery for Dummies would allow him to stay there without argument from Upley. I don't know that such was the title he took down, but since he wouldn't understand one word in fifty of any scientific treatise, it served as an example. They were the only four faces I recognised, but aside from them there were only another six or seven browsers and they soon wandered off seeking more captivating avenues of reading pleasure.

With time coming up to six, the potatoes needed peeling and Dennis's steak pie needed defrosting along with my frozen quiche, so I shut down the laptop and scanned the list of missing titles as supplied by Upley, but it told me nothing other than anyone taking out such diverse titles as *Forensic Techniques in Crime Detection*, *Embalming: Good Practice*, *Toxicity of Common Household Chemicals*, *The book of Funeral Services*, was either a trainee undertaker, priest or detective (I did not for one moment believe it was Simon) or someone who has watched too many modern and macabre murder thrillers and at the same time was cautious about the amount of bleach he poured down the sink.

Chapter Seven

Getting out of bed early was never part of my daily routine. Dennis was always up at six and gone by half past seven. I tended to see the light of day about nine-ish and I took a leisurely approach to washing, dressing, etc. followed by an equally leisurely breakfast, usually cereal and milk, and a welcome first cup of tea.

That changed on Wednesday, the twenty-second. I was up before Dennis left for work, determined to devote my full attention to stolen library books, a potential flashpoint with the Frogshaws, and a visit to Benny's Bargain Basement to speak with Barnes Junior, Barry... assuming the shop would be open for business again. And beyond that, I still needed some Christmas accoutrements for the house, not least of which was a string of tinsel for the wall clock.

The snow stopped overnight, but the sky was as dull and gloomy as the previous day, which might have indicated more of the heavenly dandruff on its way. On the other hand, the bit which stuck yesterday was all but gone, which in turn meant the temperature must have come up a degree or two. You wouldn't think so the speed with which Cappy the Cat went out, attended to his ablutions and came back in to settle in front of the fire. I wasn't persuaded either when I stepped out to get into my car.

First port of call was the library to ensure the surveillance was up and running, and after enjoying a cup of tea and inconsequential chat with Upley and Kim, mainly consisting of reporting on yesterday's non-event, I came out of the library at half past nine, had a brief debate with myself, and forgot about Benny's Bargain Basement. Instead I headed out to the Frogshaws' farm on the moors. It made sense because if the weather hit us again, I may not be able to get there. Worse, if I was already there, I might not be able to get back.

Jack Frogshaw was a small-time thug. There's one in every town. If there were any shady rackets going on in and around Haxford, it was a safe bet that he had fingers in the pie, but the mainstay of his income was from loan sharking. Not in serious amounts, because judging from the state of his farm, he didn't have two ha'pennies to rub together. He loaned out the odd fifty or hundred to those souls who were hard up, and charged usurious interest, backed up by the promise of a good hiding for those who got behind with their payments. From my days on the force, I also knew that he was suspected of selling the odd stolen car, and other, similarly stolen goods, and it wouldn't surprise me to learn that he was involved in whatever drug dealing was going on in Haxford. Not that there was much. Most of the regular dealers were well known to Mandy and her colleagues, and like the real truth about Jack Frogshaw, they were about as intimidating as a gang of schoolchildren collecting for their annual waste paper drive. I've said it before; Haxford did not do serious crime.

Most of this was going through my mind as I drove up the narrow, winding Moortop Lane, but there was something else. Jack Frogshaw's posturing as the local Mr Big might well owe more to his imagination than reality, but he was a tough nut. I was a woman alone and unlike those far off days when I routinely challenged half heads, I had no baton, only an umbrella, and there was no backup I could call upon.

Aged somewhere in his early forties, he took over the mantle from his ageing father, who was now about seventy and virtually housebound (so everyone understood). Jim Frogshaw ran the farm as a farm, but like many such establishments it barely covered the cost of his brand new Land Rover Discovery, so when he handed the reins to son Jack, they got out of sheep and into unlicensed money lending.

Tall, the slightest trace of a tub showing at his midriff, his features were set in a familiar scowl, as if that should be enough to scare off undesirables like burglars, reporters, and the police, and if I'm honest, I felt a bit jittery when I climbed out of the car, skirted round his newish Volvo saloon and faced him on his doorstep.

"Anyone accuses my lad of anything and they'll reckon with me," he warned when I asked if John was in, "and don't think that just because you're a woman it'll make any difference. I'll still knuckle you."

There are times when I can't help it. My mouth just runs away with me, and this was one of them. "Well, let's be honest, anyone with a face like yours wouldn't be able to get a woman's attention any other way, would he? No wonder they all call you Froggy."

That was a mouthful too far. He came out of the doorway and marched towards me, fists clenched, and I had to slide my brain (and mouth) into a higher gear.

"Hold on, hold on," I insisted.

"I will. I'll hold onto your throat."

"Do that and your Johnny will likely go down for a stretch."

That, at least, made him pause. "What for? He hasn't done nothing."

"You mean he hasn't done anything," I said, and silently cursed my stupid mouth for the second time. "Listen, Jack, he was in Benny Barnes's place yesterday morning when whatever happened happened—"

"And someone grassed him up. Wait while I get my hands on—"

"Just be quiet and listen." I gave him a moment to shut up and switch his ears on. "No one grassed John up. The police have him on the street cameras running from Benny's shop right after the gunshot. You know what Paddy Quinn's like. If they lay hands on John, they'll charge him with something and he'll spend Christmas with some of your old pals in Wakefield nick. Thing is, I saw that footage, and neither John nor his pal were armed, so whatever went off in the shop, probably had nothing to do with them. The only reason I came out here was to talk to your boy, see what he can tell me about what happened yesterday. And any information he gives me won't go any further."

"He didn't see nothing, he doesn't know nothing. Now get in your car and get lost, before I change my mind and rearrange your face."

I opened the car door, and glared back at him. "Will you be that brave when Quinn and his crew come knocking? Cos they're looking for John." I got in the car, turned on the ignition to let the electric window down. "If Johnny wants to talk to me, he can find me at the library first thing every morning and from about four in the afternoon." I closed the window again to shut out his cursing, started the engine and pulled away, turning left onto the lane and back down the hill towards Haxford centre.

I was still trembling but secretly proud of myself. What did I say to Upley yesterday? I don't get into confrontations. Well I did, and I came away with at least a score draw.

It was turned ten o'clock and I needed a soothing cup of tea and toasted teacake to settle my ebullient system. Terry's Tea Bar in the market hall would do nicely, and after that I would pay Barry Barnes a visit. By the time I was done with him, I should be ready to go back to the library and either check on or download the early footage from my spy camera.

As I cruised down the hill in second gear – Dennis always recommended a low gear going downhill to prevent the car running away from me – I felt the first tendrils of pleasure tingling through me. And no, I didn't mean the pleasure everyone would naturally assume I meant. I meant satisfaction… No, I meant… Well, what I meant was not what others think I might mean. It was a hint of delight derived from the last twenty-four hours of inquisitiveness. I'd never been hugely successful as a private investigator. Why would I be? I lived in Haxford and as I keep saying, it was not the crime capital of the world. It wasn't even the crime capital of West Yorkshire, and that meant customers, clients, call them what you will, were thin on the ground. I averaged three or four cases a year, so I was not exactly giving Sam Spade a run for his money. But with three days to Christmas, I had two cases on the go, even if one of them was nothing more than pure nosiness, and I was putting in the effort on both of them. I had quizzed a suspected wannabe mini-mobster and set up illegal surveillance in the library. That was good going for me.

The last case I had was a woman who wanted me to find her missing lorry driver husband. It took me the better part of three weeks, and when I did find him, she wasn't best pleased. He was on remand in Leeds on charges of serial burglary. When she went to see him, he admitted he hadn't written to her because he didn't like confessing that he was out of work, and when he went out in his overalls every night, he wasn't trucking butter, ice cream, and so on to Burton-on-Tent. He was out on the rob, breaking and entering,

Compared to that case, I was making good progress on the brouhaha at Benny's Bargain

Basement, even if I would never get paid for it, and I anticipated the library camera delivering the inside story of the stolen books this side of Christmas. As such, I was feeling dead pleased with myself.

It didn't take much to puncture the unaccustomed elation. The toasted teacake and tea at Terry's were fine – they were the best in Haxford – but then I learned that Benny's Bargain Basement was still shut, and according to rumour, Barry was still with his father (and wife and mother) at Huddersfield Royal where Benny had not yet come round. Then I hit the library and came across both Upley and Kim in a nervy mood.

There were a few browsers checking out the shelves and I could see one or two heads bowed over the form sheets in the reading room. In deference to the former, I kept my voice down. "What's wrong? Have your lottery numbers come and you've just realised you forgot to buy a ticket??"

Upley reached under the counter and came up with my mini-camera, dangling like a dead fish on a line. That's a pretty accurate analogy, because the mains wire had been torn in half between the camera and the adaptor, which, he hurried to tell me, was still where I left it, plugged into the wall socket near the Medical/Biochemistry section.

I was annoyed. Why wouldn't I be? That camera and its SD card cost me honest money. Struggling to keep my voice down, I demanded, "How did that happen?"

"Harry Kepler," Kim replied. "He spotted it plugged in at the wall, followed the lead back to the camera and climbed up on the lower shelf to take it down. But, acourse, you'd Sellotaped it to the top of the shelves, and when he tugged, the entire shelf almost fell over. As it was, a load of books fell off and tore your cable in half. Sorry, Chrissy."

Upley handed over the damaged items and assured me, "There is a positive side to this."

I was still making an effort to control my annoyance. "We caught the book thief on video?"

"Well, er, no, but we did manage to ban Kepler."

The anger was spooling up again and I know I couldn't go much longer without bringing the entire population of the library into our confidence. "For fooling around with my camera?"

"For climbing on the lower shelves, actually. It constitutes abuse of council property."

That was it. I let loose the acid and I didn't care who heard. "And never mind what he did to my property? Well, Alden, without the camera, all I can do is stay here every day and at twenty pounds an hour, it's going to cost you a lot of money. In fact by Friday, you'll probably owe me more than the value of the books you've lost."

"Please keep your voice down, Mrs Capper." I could see the panic consuming him. "There must be another way."

I was never so determined. "It's either that, or we throw the towel in now."

"Can I make a suggestion?" Kim butted in. "The internal security cameras."

She pointed up at the wall this side of the partitioned off reading room where a bog-standard security camera pointed down and into the room. I was guessing, but I think Upley wanted it that way so he could keep his irritable eye on the barflies.

By now I'd managed to regain some control over my temper. "Don't think I'm being picky, Kim, but it's keeping tabs on the reading room, and the books are being taken from the far side of the library." I pointed across the vast room to the Medical/Biochemistry shelves.

"The cameras are adjustable," she told me. "We can alter the direction it looks in, and as long as Alden is okay with it, we can let you download the footage. All we need is someone to climb up, loosen the bolts and alter the camera's angle."

It was an acceptable solution, one which mollified some of my aggrieved feelings at the loss of my spy camera's power source. I looked to Alden for his agreement, but he was obviously not persuaded. "Problem?" I asked.

"Well, yes. If we're to use our own equipment, what is the point of employing you to make inquiries? We could do it ourselves."

Kim had just talked me out of a job. Fortunately, rescue came from that same quarter when she demanded of Upley, "Since when do we have time to sit in the back room and do nothing but watch the security cameras? There's only the two of us, Alden, and we have enough to do dealing with browsers, borrowers, and putting the books back on the shelves. If you okay Chrissy to download the footage, she can study it at her leisure. Am I right or am I right?"

He made one last ditch attempt to get out of it. "We'll need to bring someone in to alter the camera.

I don't know how long the council's maintenance department will take to get round to that."

"No worries," I said, digging out my phone. "I'll get Dennis to come down. He'll be here in ten minutes."

"Yes but—"

"Alden," I interrupted, "You either want this business settled or you don't. I'll square Dennis up and add his bill to mine so the town hall won't query it. Now, do I bell him or do I go home and prepare my final invoice and leave you to your stolen books?"

He capitulated with a silent nod, and I hit the call button for my other half.

"Hey up, Chrissy, what do you want?"

"Jump in your van, Dennis, and come down to the library. I need you to realign one of their security cameras."

He was almost as bad as Upley. "That's council work, that is. Do you know how long they take to pay up?"

"You're not doing it for the council. This job is for me."

"I did a job for you the other day after you had an argument with a bollard."

"Anymore smart remarks like that and I'll find you so many jobs to do for me that you won't see the inside of your workshop this side of next Christmas. Just get yourself down here with your toolbox."

While we waited for Dennis, I ambled over to the wall socket where my mains adaptor was still plugged in. It was feeling seriously sorry for itself, the wire attached to nowhere, dangling down like a cow's thin teat with no calf to suckle on it. I wondered if a) it could be repaired and b) how long the camera would run on its own internal power and c) how I'd charge the camera up again when the battery died. Well, I knew how long it would work on its internal battery but I didn't know how I would charge that battery when it flatlined.

It was quarter past eleven when Dennis arrived and I showed him the damaged adaptor and put the repair proposition to him. "Give it here. I'll get Grimy to have a look at it. Don't look like it'll mend, but he'll tell us one way or t'other."

From there, Dennis set up his stepladder and spanners in hand, began faffing with the camera while I checked the images on Upley's computer and Kim stood at the staff room door using hand signals to tell Dennis which way I wanted the camera moving. Eventually he got it right, and as he came down the ladder with the library clock reading twenty-five to twelve, Mandy Hiscoe walked in with a uniformed constable behind her.

"Hiya, Mandy," Dennis greeted her. "Looking for books on how to detect a rotten smell in a bunged up lavatory?"

"Nice to see you, Dennis, but bog off just the same." Mandy focussed on Upley. "I'm sorry, Alden, but I'll have to ask you to come with me to the station."

It didn't only take Upley by surprise. It hit everyone. Silence like I'd never heard in my life fell over the entire library. I mean, libraries are supposed to be quiet anyway, but this wasn't just quiet, it was absolute hush on a cosmic scale. Never mind a pin drop. You could have heard the fingers parting to let it drop. This is assuming fingers make some kind of tiny, undetectable 'pop' sound when they part, and even if such was not the case, you could still have heard them parting.

Upley was the first to recover. "The police station? But I'm in the middle of a day's work. I can't just—"

"I know all that, but you will have to come with me. We have bad news, and we need to speak with you urgently."

"What kind of bad news?"

"I'd really rather not talk about it here."

"And I must insist that you do."

Mandy hovered, undecided what to do. She glanced past Upley and to the staff room. "Can we go in there?"

I had to hand it to Upley. I never thought he had much in the way of nerve, but he stood his ground. He waved a hand around the room. "Since you've already alerted everyone here to the situation, I must insist that you speak here and now."

Mandy drew in a deep breath. I knew this girl. You could only push her so far, and Upley had reached the limit. "Very well. We found your wife, Alden. Dead. She's been poisoned, and I'm arresting you on suspicion of her murder and the other killings known as the work of the Graveyard Poisoner."

Chapter Eight

Mandy's announcement was greeted with another stunned hush and finely-honed attention, and not just from the counter, Dennis and me. The rest of the browsers were tuning in, the reading room door opened, and a couple of the regular barflies were listening. It was almost as if everyone in the library had tuned in to a rendition of Hamlet's 'to be or not to be' gig.

At the counter, Kim's hand flew to her mouth. Alongside her, Upley reeled and for a moment I thought he was going to faint. Without waiting for someone to invite me, I pushed my way into the reading room, grabbed one of the chairs and rushed back to the counter with it. Kim helped Upley round, and sat him down.

"Make him some tea," I ordered. "Plenty of sugar. It's good for shock."

Kim, obviously distressed, tears forming in her eyes, rushed to obey. Mandy chose to argue.

"I don't have time for this, Chrissy."

It wasn't often that I would lose it with a police officer. I used to be one and I had nothing but respect for them. But I came close this time. "You've got it wrong, Mandy. Look at him he's in shock."

"Yes, because he's been caught out. And I need him back at the station."

"Take him like this, and he might be dead before you get there. I don't know what's going on, but it wasn't him."

"The only way you could know that is if you were there when she died and in that case, I'll have to speak to you too." She swivelled to look at my husband. "And possibly you."

"I only came here to realign the security camera," Dennis said, sounding as if he was in a hurry to distance himself from anything and everything that went on in the building.

I hurried to disabuse Mandy. "I was out at the Frogshaw's place until an hour ago, trying to get a lead on his son."

"Still chasing up the story on Benny's Bargain Basement?" Mandy asked, and I nodded by return. "That's on the back burner, Chrissy. At least until Benny comes round. This is more important, and Paddy will be in Haxford later this afternoon… probably for the duration now. If we're right, this is twice in the last month our friend has struck." She pointed a finger at Upley.

I was on the snapping point. I drew my coat about myself and said, "In that case, I shall have to look into this myself, and then it'll be me needing to speak to you."

Kim returned with a cup of tea for Upley, and Dennis chose that moment to come back from his 'don't want to know' stand. "Now, Chrissy, don't go poking your nose in."

"Dennis, get back to your work and leave me to

do mine." I faced Chrissy again. "When did Mrs Upley die?"

Still fuming, she replied. "We don't know yet, but we figure he did her sometime during the night or first thing this morning."

"And aside from poisoning, what makes you think Alden is the Graveyard Poisoner?"

It was a stupid question, but Mandy answered it anyway. "We found her in the graveyard of St Asaph's on Cottingley Road, laid out like all the other victims."

"Then that's where I'll be."

"Chrissy—"

"Shut up, Dennis."

I marched out of the library and round to the car park. The entire fiasco was absolutely outrageous. Alden Upley, the Graveyard Poisoner? I'd never heard anything so ridiculous.

It was ten minutes to twelve as I started the engine, and it occurred to me that I didn't know where Upley lived. A quick call to a tearful Kim put the matter right. Greenmount Lane. Unfortunately I didn't know where Greenmount Lane was either, and she didn't know what number they lived at.

"It'll be easy to spot, I should think. It'll be swarming with coppers."

My satnav found it and I was on my way.

West of town, south of Barncroft Memorial Park, Greenmount Lane rambled its way off Huddersfield Road for over half a mile until it joined Cottingley Road. A roundabout route to The Cottage. it was considered to be part of the 'better' quarter of Haxford, a description which might have fitted the right hand side of the road, where the houses were all 1920s and 30s semi-detached des reses with their front lawns, short drives and up and over garage doors, but the left hand side was a long terrace of old, brick built, Victorian, two up, two down houses with small front yards and rear yards, invisible to me, which were not much bigger. I knew. I grew up in such a house.

As Kim guessed, the Upleys' place was easy to pick out thanks to a large presence of SOCO and forensic boys and girls. A sprawling semi-detached house with a large front garden and a small car parked in the drive, which I guessed would be Evelyn's. I'd noticed Alden's on the car park behind the library. I sat watching for ten minutes, hoping for a sight of Simon or someone I knew well, but no such luck. I rang Mandy twice to apologise and try and calm things between us, but I got no answer. I reasoned she would be at the police station by then, interrogating Alden, possibly with Paddy Quinn at her side.

I drove further on, past a row of small, local shops on the right, and up to the T-junction with Cottingley Road where I turned right. Two hundred yards on, I came to St Asaph's, its blackened spire striking into the grim, December sky. And again I found a team of forensic officers checking out the graveyard.

I had to admit, if only to myself, that the whole episode was strange. When it came to disposing of the bodies, the Graveyard Poisoner had never repeated himself. All four victims had been found in different graveyards, and yet this was the same churchyard where he had left the body of his first victim, Oscar Longwood. There were, I decided, two possibilities. The Graveyard Poisoner had either run out of ideas or the body of Evelyn Upley had been deliberately left here to incriminate her husband. I favoured the latter, but as I thought about it, there were at least two other options. One, it really was Alden Upley and he was emulating the Graveyard Poisoner to divert suspicion, or two, the Graveyard Poisoner had been too busy over the last few weeks, and he was in a hurry when he dealt with Evelyn.

I turned round, doubled back, and drove past the Upleys' place, then pulled over on the right when I spotted a couple of neighbours standing by their gates and watching the action. Like the incident at Benny's Bargain Basement the previous day, this kind of police activity made for great entertainment.

They were both middle-aged going on elderly women, one sporting an old-fashioned flowered pinny under a thick cardigan and an early-years Coronation Street headscarf wrapped around her grey hair. The other had a red topcoat and a matching woolly bonnet. The only reason I spotted them was her red hat and coat. What with it being Christmas and all, she reminded me of Santa.

I got out of the car and ambled to them. With an air of casual inquiry, putting across the impression of a passer-by, I focussed on headscarf and pinny. "What's going on over there?"

"She's dead." Yorkshire folk never waste anything. Not even words.

Maintaining a conversational, gossipy air, still

trying to sound like a passing nosy parker, I said, "The church on Cottingley Road is alive with police, too."

"That's where they found her," headscarf and pinny assured me.

Mrs Santa joined in. "You're thinking it'll be one for your blog, Mrs Capper?"

It's a cross I had to bear, what with me being fairly well-known in and around Haxford. I found it impossible to work incognito. "Nothing of the kind. If you follow my vlog, you'll know that I don't do anything controversial, but I'm always looking for the human interest story."

Mrs Santa pressed on. "Aye, well, she's dead. Deserves it, mind. God, she were a miserable old sow, she were."

"True enough," said headscarf and pinny. "Wouldn't even pass the time of day, she wouldn't. I walked past on me way back from the shops this morning and she was putting the bins out, so I said, 'good morning' to her and do you know what she said? Nothing. Not a word. Just stuck her snooty nose in the air and went back in."

Alarm bells rang in my head. "This morning? What time would that be?"

"I thought you were looking for human interest?"

I smiled sweetly at headscarf and pinny. "I like to get my facts straight."

This seemed suspicious to Mrs Santa. "Will you be naming us on your video doings?"

"Not if you don't want me to."

"We don't."

Now that Mrs Santa made their joint opposition

to identification clear, I was compelled to ignore her and concentrate on headscarf and pinny. "You were telling me the time you went to the shops."

"It'd be, what? After nine o'clock. I don't go to t'shops until the kids are all in school."

The obvious occurred to me right away. "The kids are off school. Christmas holidays."

"Aye, well, I don't alter my routine to suit t'education department."

As far as they were concerned, that appeared to be the end of the discussion, so I thanked them and made my way back to the car thinking that Ena Sharples and Elsie Tanner would have nothing on this pair. Not that I was really old enough to remember Ena and Elsie, both of whom checked out of Corrie while I was in my teens. At that age I had other areas of interest.

Settling behind the wheel of my car again, I made a note of the house numbers, then started the engine and debated with myself on the best way of approaching the police. Kim had called it right and they were wrong. I didn't know who was responsible for the death of Evelyn Upley, but it wasn't her husband. I tried Mandy again, and got the familiar voicemail. Well, if Mandy wouldn't come to the phone, the phone would have to go to Mandy.

It's surprising just how quickly time passes when you're so busy. An hour back, I was in the library arguing over my broken camera and now here I was fighting my way back into town to clear Alden Upley's name.

Fighting was an adequate description. There

were just three days to Christmas, and didn't Haxford know about it? The northern half of the bypass was heaving with cars, vans, lorries, and buses, and with my usual forethought and planning, after battling and crawling along with nose to tail traffic reminiscent of Tuesday morning, I had to make a right turn into the police station. Would the oncoming traffic give way? Not this side of Easter Sunday it wouldn't.

I must have waited almost five minutes before a rare gentleman driver paused and let me cross, and during that interval, I checked my indicators time and again, but according to the dashboard I was definitely signalling to turn right. Why hadn't I headed south from Greenmount and cut through the streets to come at the police station from the opposite direction? It would have saved me at least two or three minutes. The delay made me pine for the days when I had lemon and white stripes and flashing blue lights. On the car, obviously. I'm no fashion icon, but even I wouldn't wear lemon and white stripes. In Ibiza, maybe, but not Haxford, especially in December.

I hurried into the station and came up against the formidable presence of Sergeant Vic Hillman on reception. We were probationers together and consequently knew each other of old. He approved when I gave up the police, but it went deeper than that. I was the one who nicknamed him Minx. To be truthful, it was mostly Dennis's fault. He was always going on about some old car called the Hillman Minx, and another model named the Hillman Imp. Considering Vic was something like six feet six in his bare feet, I thought that Imp didn't quite fit, so I called him Minx, and it stuck. He never really forgave me for that, and right then, he wasn't impressed when I demanded to see either Mandy or Quinn.

"They're both busy so clear off."

"It's urgent," I insisted. "Come on, Minx, you know I don't waste police time."

"You wasted eight years of police time before you jacked it in. Now—"

I cut him off. "I know that Mandy and possibly Paddy are interviewing Alden Upley, and I have information for them. It's urgent, and if I don't get a word with them, you'll be in trouble when they do get to me. Now, please, bell Mandy or Paddy and tell them I need to speak to them."

He aimed his ballpoint at the benches opposite. "Wait over there. I'll let 'em know you're here."

I did as he told me, and sat down to wait for one or other of the detectives appearing. I would have preferred Mandy, but as it turned out, I got Paddy Quinn and he was in a proper paddy.

"What do you want, Christine? We're busy—"

By now, I was more than a little fraught and I cut him off. "Alden Upley did not kill his wife. She was still alive at half past nine this morning, and he was in the library at that time."

My announcement had the effect of bringing him up short, and it helped cool me down.

"What?"

"You heard. Evelyn Upley was still alive between nine and half past this morning and Kim will testify that Alden was in the public library from half past eight onwards. I was with Alden for an hour from about a quarter to eleven, and he was still in the library when Mandy came rushing in to arrest him."

It was as if I hadn't said a word. "And how do you know Evelyn was still alive then? According to us, he killed her sometime last night or maybe early this morning."

I took out my little notebook. "I did something you probably haven't got round to. I spoke to a couple of the Upleys' neighbours, and one of them spoke to Evelyn sometime between nine and half past."

Sweat began to break out on his brow. "Yeah but these people always answer questions with daydreams, don't they?"

"I didn't ask questions. I chatted with them. It's what we women are best at. Gossip. You should know. You're the one who first told me that's all we women are good for."

I expected him to react to my goading, but he didn't. Instead, he began to dig deep. "She could be mistaken about the time. This neighbour, I mean."

I shook my head and entertaining a mental image of headscarf and pinny said, "Not this woman. She told me she'd been to the shops and they probably don't open until after Alden has left for work. Use your nut and get someone out to speak to her. I don't know her name, but she lives at 98 Greenmount Lane, and her neighbour at number 100 will confirm it."

I thought I'd heard all the possible swearwords in the English language, but Paddy came out with a string of invective, some of which I didn't recognise. I do know that before most of the nouns there were an awful lot of words ending in 'ing' and most of them were unsuitable for mixed company or the ears of children.

He half turned to walk away, and cast a glare over his shoulder. "You wait there. I want a full statement from you on everything you know."

As it turned out, it was a wait of over ten minutes, and thankfully, he sent Mandy out to deal with me. Paddy Quinn did not have exclusive rights to irritability and if I had to deal with him much more, I would have pleaded extreme provocation for beating him to a pulp on the black floor tiles.

Our earlier disagreement was forgotten and Mandy showed no trace of chagrin at my having cleared Upley. She took all the details and confirmed that officers had been sent to Geenmount Lane to speak to headscarf and pinny and Mrs Santa.

"So you'll be releasing Alden?"

"As and when we've had confirmation of your story, probably. Why?" She laughed. "Don't tell me you're getting sweet on him, Chrissy."

"Don't be silly. Mind you, I think Kim might be a bit that way. She was really distressed when you came to arrest him. I'm on my way back to the library when I've done with you. Make sure she's all right." A thought occurred to me. "You won't be closing the place, will you?"

"We thought about it, but we don't have enough scientific bods to go round, and now that you've all but cleared Alden's name, there's no point." She shook her head, sadly. "I told Paddy we were jumping the gun, but you know him. Orders are orders and he ordered Alden arrested. What could I do? Now we have to back off, console the poor guy and let him get back to work."

"Oh, I don't think he'll be fit to work."

"Well, he can't go home. Our people are all over the place there and even if he's innocent – which I don't doubt for one minute – we still have to go through it with a fine tooth comb."

"On which point, I'll leave you with it, Mandy. Keep me informed, won't you?"

Her laughter was grudging. "You've blown him out of the water once, so Paddy will likely tell me to keep you out of it, but I'll keep you up to date, and thanks, Chrissy."

From there, I made my way back to the library and as I paid for my parking, an ancient, maroon van pulled into the car park. The rattling engine stopped and there was the familiar raking sound of a handbrake drawn up through its ratchet.

I knew that vehicle, which just goes to show that I did listen to Dennis now and then. It was a 1946 Morris Y12 10cwt van and it belonged to the Shuttle family. Dennis did the MOT preparation work on it every year. A labour of love for him, but a *paying* labour of love all the same. I wasn't aware that it was still on the road. In fact, I recall Dennis telling me that last year, and for some time this year, it was in need of a major overhaul and off the road for a long time. It belonged to Bob Shuttle, but he went wandering a few years ago, and he'd never been seen since, and given their age, I felt it unlikely that Patience, Faith or Charity would be driving it.

I reassessed that opinion when Patience Shuttle climbed unsteadily out of the van, collected her shopping bag from the passenger seat and with a smile, came slowly towards me.

"Good morning, Patience," I greeted her.

"I think you'll find it's afternoon, Christine."

Patience obviously short on patience, I thought to myself. "How on earth do you manage driving that van?"

"Oh, you young'uns. You don't know you're born. During the war we were driving lorries, me and my sisters."

I knew this was so much twaddle. The three sisters were all in their early eighties, and they would have been babies or at best toddlers when war broke out. I put it down to the rambling of old minds, and said, "I thought Bob did all your running about."

"Aye, but he's not here anymore, is he, and I'm the only one with a driving licence." She changed the subject. "Have you heard about young Alden's wife?"

How anyone could describe Alden Upley as 'young' was a question I put to one side. Preferring not to tell Patience of my adventures in the Greenmount Lane area, I said, "I was here when the police arrested him."

She grunted. "Surprised he didn't do it sooner. Terrible woman. If you had a cat like her, you'd put it down."

Patience obviously had no worries about

speaking ill of the dead.

Still unwilling to tell her what I'd learned, I said, "It's only a suspicion. There's nothing to say he did it."

"Aye, well... if he didn't he should have done." Patience tutted. "I don't know what this town's coming to, I don't. Well, better get on." She shuffled off to the library and I shook my head in bewilderment. Dotty old bat, I thought to myself. Like most towns and cities, Haxford had been in decline since... well, as far back as I could remember.

I followed her into the building and Kim left the work to a colleague brought in at short notice from the town hall, while she and I got together in the staff room where I brought her up to speed.

"He can stay with me," she said when I told her he wouldn't be able to go home.

My eyebrows rose. "Oh, yes?"

Kim tutted by return. "What are you like? You know full well I've got a spare room after Wayne did a runner last year."

My slight air of disbelief must have been clear from my face. It wasn't that I seriously believed there was anything between them, but I never thought Kim felt that highly of Upley. When I said as much, she was quick to correct me.

"You don't know him, Chrissy. Not like I do. I know he can be a bit hoity-toity, I know he's a pain in the bottom when he wants, but there are other sides to him. Things that you don't know about. You remember I was half an hour late yesterday, after the traffic jam on the High Street? I asked if he wanted me to make up the extra time, and he told me to forget it. If the town hall didn't know – and they didn't – they couldn't complain. And when my mum took poorly last year, he gave me two days' compassionate leave to go to Leeds and see her. I wasn't entitled to it. I'd had all my leave for the year. And he gave me a bottle of Irish Cream for my birthday. Somewhere under all that, that…"

She was struggling for the correct word. "Severity? Nit-picking? Stuffiness?"

"Yeah. Whatever. Somewhere under all that, he's a good man."

"I'll take your word for it, Kim. For now, I've got other things I need to get on with. Can I leave you to it or do you want me to wait until he comes back?"

"No, Chrissy. You get off. I'll ring you later."

There was little I could do on any investigative front until four o'clock when I had to return to the library to pick up the day's video footage, so I ambled along the High Street, called into Warrington's bakery where I paid for a couple of cream cakes, and then drove home.

I wanted every scrap of information I could find on the Graveyard Poisoner.

Chapter Nine

You'd think that Cappy the Cat would be pleased to see me, but not so. When I walked into the house, he was spark out on the settee. He opened one eye, realised it was me, and shut the eye again to go back to dreaming of chasing mice, overdosing on catnip, fouling next door's lawn, or whatever cats dreamt about. He perked up when I made myself a cup of tea and settled down with one of Warrington's cakes, but I wasn't fooled. His interest was focussed on the cake's layers of cream.

Leaving him cream and crumbs on the plate, I booted up the laptop and Googled Haxford Graveyard Poisoner. The knowledge, as I expected, amounted to a little bit over nothing, but if the Graveyard Poisoner had successfully avoided the combined efforts of the police and forensic scientists, there was plenty of information on the victims, most of it coming from the police via the Haxford Recorder.

I knew Ian Noiland, the Recorder's editor quite well. Because I was a fairly well-known blogger and vlogger, there was a history of two-way contact between us. Quite often, I would ring him for background material for my pieces, and just as often, he would call me for confirmation of this, that, or the other. The cheeky so-and-so also got in touch now and again in an effort to sell me advertising. I invariably told him where to go. "I'm popular enough, thank you, Ian."

But I was hesitant to call him on the Graveyard Poisoner. Like everyone else, he would be bogged down with Christmas cacophony and the breaking news of the (supposed) latest victim. Instead, I concentrated on the information I could pick up from the paper's website, and there was plenty in the archives for me to go at.

Oscar Aldwych Longwood was the Graveyard Poisoner's first known victim, and that was two years ago. Although I didn't know Oscar personally, he was quite a character, especially when it came to explaining his curious middle name. He insisted that the tale was family hearsay, but that didn't stop him from repeating it. His parents christened him so because he was conceived during an air raid in 1940, when his mother and father sheltered in Aldwych underground station.

I recalled telling Dennis the tale, and he was incredulous. "Those underground stations were choc-a-bloc with people; they were kipping on the platform, the track, everywhere. How the bejeebers did his mam and dad get it together with all those people round them?"

"You'd be surprised what a man and a woman can get up to even in a crowd," I said to him, and his eyebrows shot up to his hairline.

"Oh, aye. And how would you know?"

I tapped the side of my nose. "Ask no questions, get no lies told."

Oscar was seventy-eight years of age when his body was found in the graveyard of St Asaph's on Cottingley Road, not far from where he lived. He was laid out on an overgrown, unkempt and untended grave. His arms were crossed, as if waiting for the casket to arrive and the service to begin. The police did not immediately treat it as a suspicious death. With a history of dropping out of sight for days at a time, he had been missing two days before he was found, and the police assumed that he was an old man who must have come to a situation where he was expecting to expire, so he lay down on the grave and prepared himself for eternity.

The theory was tenuously supported by a routine check on the grave's current residents from which they learned he was not related to any of them. A widower, his wife had died several years previously, and she had been cremated, and her funeral service was not held at St Asaph's. Further research indicated that he had absolutely nothing to do with the church. When the police dug deeper and deeper into his background, they learned that he was a dyed-in-the-wool atheist whose only forays into churches of any description were to attend weddings, christenings, and funerals, and even then it was only to grab his share of free drinks, or gloat over those he had outlived.

Matters were complicated further when the post-mortem results came through, revealing that he had been poisoned; strychnine. Oscar was a lifelong smoker, and any intake of strychnine would severely attack his respiratory system as well as sending him into muscular spasms. He had ingested a sizeable amount, but it was mixed with beer, Haxford Best Bitter to be precise, and in a man of that age, the police concluded that he would hardly notice the bitter taste of strychnine.

I begged leave to doubt that. Oscar may very well have been conceived in London, but he was a Haxford man, and they were a notoriously fickle breed. If they demanded Haxford Best Bitter and you tried fobbing them off with, say, John Smith's, you would reap the whirlwind. If I was right about Oscar Longwood, he would have noticed any contaminant in his ale.

And yet, he appeared peaceful in death, which supported the theory that it was either suicide or that he didn't notice the strychnine. As I read the report, I came to a different conclusion. I concluded that his killer had manipulated his face before rigor mortis set in, and made it appear that he was content with his end.

The vicar of St Asaph's insisted that Oscar's body was not there at ten o'clock the previous night, and the pathologist confirmed the time of death as about midnight. That meant his killer had the audacity to bring the body to the graveyard either in the early hours, or broad daylight. Considering he was murdered in July, no matter what time the killer brought the body to the church, he would have been visible. The road outside the church was one of those ever-busy suburban byways which led to The Cottage in a roundabout way. And yet, there was nothing in the way of tyre prints or footprints to hint at the killer's identity.

When the path report came through, the police changed their minds, and called it murder. Pathology revealed that he had been crudely embalmed, which prompted an immediate investigation into the local funeral directors. That came to nothing, as might be expected. Theirs was a macabre trade (someone had to do it) but they treated cadavers with great respect and to a man, woman and enterprise, they insisted they would have done a much more professional job than had been carried out on Oscar.

Forensic efforts at the graveyard yielded no clues to the killer. Whoever was behind it had taken extreme care to leave absolutely no traces of himself. The body had been washed and the only other item that came from the pathologist's examination was a criss-cross pattern at various locations on the body where fingerprints might have been found. The conclusion was that the perpetrator had worn freely-available washing-up gloves.

Testimony from those who knew Oscar said he was a bitter, lonely old man, his short temper exacerbated by the death of his wife, but one commentator insisted that his wife's passing left Oscar with no one upon whom he could vent his permanent state of irritation.

"He was a nasty, crabby old git," said the landlord of the Ferret Inn, refusing to abide by the time-honoured principle of not speaking ill of the dead. It later transpired that Oscar owed about fifteen pounds on his slate.

There were similarities between Oscar and victim number two, Arthur Rumbelow. He was seventy-five years of age when his body was found in the municipal cemetery attached to Haxford Chapel and Crematorium. He was killed in the November after Oscar Longwood's death. He, too, was a widower, his wife having died the previous year, and he, too, had been poisoned, and once again, the toxin was strychnine, a lot of it, which must have put him through seven kinds of hell before he finally expired.

But not necessarily, said the pathologist, having found a large bump on the back of Arthur's head which was definitely ante-mortem, i.e. before he died. That begged an immediate question; how did they get poison down him if he was unconscious. The answer came further down the report, but it was no more than intelligent guesswork. Arthur drank the stuff, realised what he'd done, and probably tried to gorge it back up, whereupon the perpetrator clouted him on the back of the head to prevent Arthur avoiding the inevitable.

An unnamed detective, commenting on the case, said Arthur appeared to have been clattered with a meat hammer, a wooden mallet used for tenderising steak. I made a note to check with Mandy on that.

Other comments revealed that Arthur was as different to Oscar as his death was similar. Still feeling the passing of his wife after almost fifty years of marriage, he maintained a cheerful and outgoing approach to life. A regular at the Woolcombers where he enjoyed a few beers and a game of darts or dominoes with friends, his neighbours said that only when he was alone at home, did he go down. His only son, a serving NCO in some army regiment, confirmed it. After Arthur's wife passed on, the son and his wife had invited Arthur to live with them in Berkshire where the son was stationed as a Permanent Staff Instructor, but Arthur wouldn't have it. He was a Haxforder through and through. The son, his wife and their teenage children were all eliminated from the inquiry on the grounds that they were over two hundred miles away at the time, something later confirmed by neighbours in Aldershot, and the sergeant's CO.

No one could account for Arthur's movements after leaving the Woolcombers at eleven the previous night, but as well as strychnine, his stomach contained undigested remnants of fish & chips, so it was a safe bet that he'd called at the Haxford Chippy, not far from the pub, although none of the crew could remember him.

I was slightly puzzled as to how Arthur came to drink the stuff. He must have smelled it the moment he brought it up to his mouth, but the Recorder hinted that he suffered from a condition called congenital anosmia; he was born without a sense of smell. The Recorder didn't say where they got the information.

The first thing the pathologist looked for was the presence of embalming fluid, but there was none and the police assumed that too little time had elapsed between his disappearance and his turning up in the cemetery, which just goes to show what our police knew about the process. Five minutes of research told me that professionals could complete the embalming process inside two hours. He was found in the same position as Oscar, i.e. laid flat on a grave with his hands crossed as if he was waiting for some kind of funeral service, and (another similarity to Oscar) he was not related to any of the people named on the gravestone. The police gave out that last snippet of information after confirming it with Arthur's son.

In need of some attention, Cappy the Cat walked all over my laptop keyboard and shut the browser down. It's something he did quite often and while Dennis always said I was daft, I still think the cat knew how to do it so I would concentrate on him.

I took a break to let him out and watched him jump over the fence into the Timmins's back garden, then switched on the kettle to make a fresh cup of tea. While I waited for it to boil, my phone rang. It was Dennis and the news was neutral. There was good and there was bad.

"Grimy's had a dekko at your mains thingy for the camera, and it's shot. Dead. RIP, adaptor. But he reckons he can get you a replacement for a fiver."

"Clean? I mean, it's not stolen or anything."

"I don't think so. Course, you never know with him, and he did say you won't get a guarantee with it."

"Does he guarantee the work he does for Jamal Patel?"

"That's different. He charges Jammy a lot more than a fiver. Hey, and while I think on, don't forget I'll want paying for that job at the library."

"Just make sure they're family prices, Dennis. And bring me that adaptor."

I cut the call and sank into my memories of two years ago and the hoo-hah after Arthur Rumbelow's murder.

POLICE STUMPED, screamed a banner headline from the Recorder about a week after the discovery of Arthur's body. A WASTE OF TAXPAYER'S MONEY was one of Ian Noiland's more vitriolic leaders, in which he castigated CID for their lack of progress on not only Arthur's death but also Oscar's.

It was the main topic of conversation in the workplaces, shops, cafés and pubs, and for all I knew, several bookies. There were those people in Haxford – Kepler, for example – who would bet on anything, including where and when the Graveyard Poisoner would strike next, and there were plenty of bookies willing to lay odds on such bets. At Haxford Fixers, it was the sole topic of discussion, with (according to Dennis) Tony Wharrier leading the campaign for the re-introduction of capital punishment, and Lester Grimes countering with a plea for compassion. Not that Lester was for or against capital punishment. He arbitrarily took the opposing stand to Tony on any issue. If Tony argued for patience and understanding of the killer's disturbed state of mind, Lester would call for a firing squad or better still, hanging, drawing, and quartering.

Ever the moderate, I kept my distance from the subject when writing my blog posts or recording my vlogs, other than closing with advice to elderly people, particularly men, to take care when they were out late at night. It was something which appeared at odds with nationwide advice telling women to be wary late at night, and I received one or two comments to that effect.

As now, Arthur's death happened in the run up to Christmas and unlike Arthur, the subject died a natural death, buried amongst the welter of yuletide interests. Haxford, the small potatoes of crime, reverted to its natural status, and the Graveyard Poisoner, who had not yet been so named, was a statistical blip and nothing more.

With a fresh cup of tea, and Cappy the Cat back indoors and snoozing in front of the fire, I returned to my laptop, opened the browser again, and continued reading.

Opinions changed when the Graveyard Poisoner struck again in August the following year.

This time, the victim was 85-year-old George Dalston, and unlike the previous pair, he was not a widower but a lifelong, gay bachelor, although he had only come out about five years before his death.

His body was found in the graveyard of Haxford Parish Church and this time it really was planted in broad daylight. A reliable witness (unnamed but identity probably known to the police) saw three people moving what looked like a shrouded body on a trolley along the narrow alley which ran to the left of the church. The witness thought no more about it at the time, believing it to be intended for the chapel of rest of a funeral parlour in one of the back streets adjacent to the alley. He changed his mind and called into the police station when the body was discovered by a woman bringing flowers to the cemetery. Legend had it that George Dalston had been laid to rest, arms crossed, on her husband's grave causing her some distress and no little inconvenience. "Those flowers cost me a flaming fortune," she was reported to have said. That's Haxford for you. Think of the cost.

Beyond his bachelorhood and sexual orientation, there were no significant differences between George's murder and the preceding pair. Strychnine was the toxin, and this time it was swamped with a cheap sherry which, so George's friends confirmed, was one of his favourite pre-dinner tipples. For a man of his age, he was fit and healthy, something attributed to his habit of walking at least two miles every day. He was neither depressed nor lonely, but enjoyed the company of a medium sized circle of friends amongst Haxford's gay community. Those friends were all quickly eliminated from police inquiries.

Like Oscar Longwood, George had not been seen for a few days, but his friends testified that there was nothing odd about that. He had friends all over Yorkshire and further afield. As a final note, the pathologist confirmed the presence of formaldehyde and water, the basis of embalming fluid, in his blood stream.

There was nothing to suggest that the police doubted the same killer was responsible for all three deaths, but they never said so in public. The Haxford Recorder, however, had no such reservations, and the early evening edition from the day Dalston was murdered blazed with the headline, GRAVEYARD POISONER STRIKES AGAIN. From that moment, the killer became known by his soubriquet.

As an ex-police officer, I knew slightly more than the Recorder, or let's put it this way; I knew slightly more than the Recorder was willing to admit to knowing.

By this time, the killer had struck three times and met the official criteria for a serial killer. Haxford born and bred Paddy Quinn may have been the man on the ground, but behind him there would be a Major Incident Team, and absolutely no stone would be left unturned in the search for the killer. I had never been questioned, but that was probably because I didn't know any of the victims. I knew, however, that detectives had called at Haxford Fixers asking routine questions of Dennis, Tony and Lester. Had anyone brought a large-ish vehicle in for service or repair, had anyone bought a large-ish vehicle from them, had anyone pestered them for substances which were potentially toxic, did they store large quantities of pesticides which might contain strychnine, and so on.

Large-ish vehicles was too vague for Dennis's liking. He serviced and carried out repairs to any number of vans and trucks, from small runabouts to heavy lorries, but all the drivers/owners were well known to him and his partners. Haxford Fixers' sales of second hand vehicles were noticeable by their infrequency, and a quick check of the books revealed they had not sold any form of commercial vehicle in the previous two or three years.

As in the aftermath of Arthur Rumbelow's death, the fuss died down, Haxford went back to sleep and aside from occasional, passing mentions in the

Haxford Recorder, the Graveyard Poisoner was forgotten.

Until about a month ago, when victim number four, Herbert Pickles, turned up in the graveyard of St Cross church on Mafeking Avenue.

The area comprised one of Haxford's three council estates, and Herbert lived not far from the church. Eighty-one years old, a widower for almost a decade, fully reconciled to his wife's passing, his neighbours described him as likeable, peaceable, a pleasure to talk to.

According to his next door neighbour, on the night of his death, Herbert left the house at half past eight to walk down to The Fleece Inn on the edge of the estate. He never got there. A group of children playing on open fields around The Fleece saw him climb into what they described as an old banger but none could identify the make of car or the model and they had no idea of the registration. Their testimony was given little credence by the police.

Strychnine was the toxin once again, but this time, there was nothing else in his stomach other than coffee, which he must have drunk with the poison, but there were signs that he'd been forced to drink it; pressure marks on his hands where he must had been compelled to hold the cup, and around his mouth where he had been force fed the poison. Once again, there were no fingerprints and the body had been thoroughly washed and sanitised, basic embalming fluid pumped into the veins before being left to lie in state on an old, communal grave in a dusty corner of the St Cross churchyard.

Outcry, clamour, hubbub, led by the Recorder

once again, and while the police went quietly about their business, it gradually calmed down, soon overtaken by the end of the month and the approach of the Christmas season. Peace once more descended on Haxford.

But now, today, the Graveyard Poisoner had struck again and he had stepped out of line with the murder of Evelyn Upley.

Why the change? Four times the Graveyard Poisoner had struck, four times it was against an elderly man leading a solitary life. Evelyn Upley was not a man – well, I assumed as much – and neither was she elderly. Alden was a year or two older than me, and it was another fairly safe assumption that his wife was of a similar age, therefore, middle aged, not elderly.

It seemed like a lot of people knew about Alden and his wife. Until earlier today when Mandy arrested him, I didn't even know he was married, let alone hitched to a dragon, so could it be then, that Alden really did murder his wife? All right, Evelyn was still alive when he was on duty at the library, but was it possible that he had put the poison in the milk, say, so that when she made herself a cuppa or a bowl of porridge, she would drop dead.

But in that case, who moved her to St Asaph's graveyard?

I decided I would need to speak with Mandy, see what she could tell me, but it would probably have to wait until the following day.

My mind drifting, trying to see the big picture, I shut down the laptop, looked out through the windows on December darkness, and with a shock realised it was turned four o'clock. I was supposed to be at the library ten minutes ago.

Chapter Ten

I broke not only the speed limit and the rule of a lifetime (certainly my recent lifetime) but also the law (again) by speaking to Kim on the smartphone as I sped down Moor Road towards town. And it was not hands-free. My car was not set up for hands-free. I'd pestered Dennis time and time again, but he said it was down to Lester Grimes – Haxford Fixers' theoretical electrical wizard – and Lester hadn't found the time. What Dennis really meant was Lester didn't like working for nothing and Dennis could be relied upon not to pay him for the job, at least not at company rates.

"I'd pay him as a guvvy, but I'm not tipping up full whack for it," Dennis once told me.

'Guvvy' was an old Yorkshire slang word for a cash job done outside the firm's time, usually without the boss' knowledge or blessing. It's what tradesmen in most walks of life and other parts of the country would call a 'foreigner', the kind of back pocket payment which the taxman never got to know about. And Dennis knew all about guvvies. He did his share when he worked for Addison's, and even now, I'm not sure that all his work went through the Haxford Fixers' books.

Kim was not a happy bunny when I got through

to her. "It's turned quarter past four, Chrissy, and you know what Alden's like. The doors are shut, bolted and alarmed at ten seconds past half past. In fact, he's making his rounds right now, chucking the punters out. You'll never make it."

"You can't hang about another fifteen minutes, Kim?"

"Wouldn't bother me, but he won't have it, especially the state he's in, and I'm only an assistant. I don't have any keys."

I had to accelerate my thinking as fast as I accelerated the car. "Listen, Kim, you must have a spare memory stick kicking about the place."

"Technically, officially, no. They're supposed to be banned to stop people downloading stuff off the web. Come on, Chrissy, you know the rules as well as anyone."

And I did. Users were supposed to ask for printouts if they wanted anything from the web, and of course, the library charged 50p per sheet for printouts. And there was I thinking public libraries were not about making money. "Kim," I pleaded, "I need that download if I'm ever gonna find your book thief. Think of it this way. Alden must be really low right now. If I could pin down your thief, it would lift him a tiny bit, wouldn't it?"

She was persuaded. "Let me have a scout about. As I say, we're not supposed to have any memory sticks on site, but Alden's completely out of it this afternoon. He's running on autopilot. I'll bet there's a couple knocking about somewhere."

"Well, if you find one, do me a favour and download this afternoon's security video. I'll get the memory stick back to you tomorrow."

"Okey-dokey. Where do you wanna meet? Car park behind us or would you fancy a snifter?"

"What about Alden? I thought he was going to stay with you."

"He has to nip home first and pick up some clean clothing. The cops'll let him do that, surely?"

"I should think so," I said even though I hadn't the faintest idea whether they would. "Anyway, I don't drink while I'm driving, but a glass of lemonade in the Tavern wouldn't come amiss. I'll go straight there and it's my round. What will I get you?" The Tavern was familiar Haxford shorthand for the Market Tavern, which as its name suggested, was attached to one end of the indoor market hall.

"Bacardi and Coke. What else? I'll see you there in twenty minutes, give or take."

The Market Tavern had this olde worlde sound to its name, but the truth was more mundane. I just about remembered them building it in the mid-seventies at the same time as they were rebuilding the market hall, which burned down one deep and crisp and even January night. It was never proved, but the general consensus was that one of the traders was hovering on the point of bankruptcy and the subsequent insurance claim solved his problem, while creating untold headaches for his fellow stallholders and the council.

As an afterthought, there was nothing particularly old about the pub the Tavern replaced, either. Edwardian, so my research told me.

The pub was never exceptionally busy at this time of the late afternoon, but with Christmas imminent it was packed, and by the time I was served, Kim had already slotted herself into a corner table and told others that the seat opposite was taken. If getting served was difficult, joining Kim was just as bad, if not worse. I had to wriggle my way through office workers knocked off from work, shoppers with hands full of bags, the occasional pair of overalls, many of them displaying the logo of Haxford Borough Council, and one clown propping up a real, four-foot Christmas tree under one hand and hold a foaming pint in the other. From speakers dotted around the walls came Christmas caterwauling – Hark the Heralds, I think – but that was drowned out by the clatter of Christmas laughter and chatter, and from outside the pub we could hear the distant strains of the Salvation Army band belting out O Come All Ye faithful… I think.

I let out a sigh of relief as I finally sat with Kim. She handed over a memory stick and took a belt of neat Bacardi.

"Aah, that hit the spot," she breathed before slopping a dash of Coke into the glass. She leaned forward. "Listen, Chrissy, Alden doesn't know nothing about that." She aimed a finger at the memory stick. "I found it in his desk. It's thirty-two gig and there were already some files on it. Dunno what they are cos I didn't have time to look, but there was just enough room to fit the afternoon's video on. I've gotta have it back first thing in the morning just in case he misses it. I don't wanna upset him any more than he's already setup."

Setup? She meant upset, of course. "No worries, Kim I'll download it when I get home, and then delete it from the memory stick."

"Well, for god's sake, don't wipe the other files out. For all I know, they might be his living will or something. Mind you, the state he's in, he probably won't notice it's missing, and if he says something, I have a good excuse. Another book went missing sometime today."

I took a sip of ice cold lemonade and relished the thirst-quenching bite. "From the Medical/Biochemistry section?"

"Nope. Religion and Phisolophy." She screwed up her face into something resembling… I don't know what, but it was straining. "A Compendialbum of Funeral Practices."

"A compendium of funeral Practices?" I asked in an effort to correct her. I loved this girl as one of my best friends, but there were times when I had to wonder how she got her job.

"That's it. What's a compendi-doings?"

"Like an encyclopaedia."

"Well why don't they just call it an enbikeclopaedia, then?"

My suspicions came to a head. Kim could be fairly obtuse, but she was not usually that slow-witted. I looked from her down at the glass of Bacardi, and then back at her. "Has that gone to your head?"

"No." She went all defensive on me and then relented. Digging in her handbag, she showed me the neck of a half bottle of vodka. "This might have done, though."

I frowned. "Drinking on duty, Kim? That's not like you."

"Partly down to Alden, poor man. We had a circular from the council the other week warning us to watch the heating on account of the price of gas going through the roof. Well, you know what Alden's like. Always got to be seen to do as he's told and then go one step further. Well, ever since we got the instruction, he's been turning the thermostat down by one degree every day. I'm not kidding, Chrissy, it was flaming freezing in there yesterday. I'm surprised you didn't notice. And I knew it'd be colder today, so I brought a bottle in to keep me warm. Anyway, after what happened I needed something, and it's Christmas, innit, and he never takes me for a Christmas drink or nothing like the other department bosses do, so what's wrong with taking a nip at work?"

"Well there are only the two of you. You can hardly throw an office party, can you?" I made an effort to cheer her up. "Think of it this way. If Alden took you for a couple of drinks, he might want more than a glass of Haxford Bitter."

Kim giggled. "The state he's in? He'd never do it. And there was I thinking you knew him. He's totally tied to his missus."

"Was totally tied to her. She's dead, remember." My comment cast an immediate air of gloom over us. "How is he? Bearing up?"

Kim toyed with her glass. "Coping. You know. The old stiff upper lip, but he keeps breaking down and crying. I'll look after him, Chrissy."

The remark only fired my suspicions again. To avert them, I said, "I didn't even know he was married."

"He was with Evelyn for more years than was good for him, I reckon. But he's a good husband... sorry, was a good husband."

Conscious of the time, I bolted down my lemonade. "I'll have to go, Kim. I have to wade through this afternoon's video if I'm gonna get this back to you for nine in the morning." I kissed the memory stick as I got to my feet. "I'll see you first thing."

It's always surprised me how quickly time passed. I came out of the Tavern just as the market hall clock was striking the quarter hour. A dainty, animated piece, where two medieval figures come out and struck the bell, it was salvaged from the fire which decimated the original market hall and the council decided to reinstate it on the new building. At that moment, it wasn't doing anything to cheer me up. Quarter past five? How could I have got this far behind schedule?

And I needed a stroll along the High Street before I could go home. I was getting as far behind with my Christmas decs as I was the book thief and Graveyard Poisoner.

I nipped into Poundland where I picked up several strands of multi-coloured tinsel and a range of tasty little reindeer, Santas, fairies and the like, as well as a pack of six, tiny, battery operated tea lights. Those would slot nicely into the open back of a little china cottage which I could set under the television. They'd make it look as if there's light coming from the cottage windows and I could already imagine a family sitting down to their Christmas meal in the warmth and comfort of their home, shielded from the elements... all of which reminded me to pick up some cotton wool balls to make fake snow.

I went into the shop with the intention of spending no more than a couple of pounds, but when I got to the checkout, I learned I didn't have enough cash to cover the fifteen-pound bill, so I used my debit card, and then crossed the street to the ATM outside the Haxford Building Society, where I drew another fifty.

I always felt guilty about that. There were those people in Haxford, people like Kepler and Rita Nuffield, who lacked the luxury of drawing extra cash when they needed it. I wouldn't say Dennis and I were well off, but we were comfortable. Many people were not, and as a sop to my conscience, I dropped a pound in the hat of a theoretically homeless man squatting on the pavement further along the street. His dog gave a couple of half-hearted wags of the tail, and as I delivered a thin, indulgent smile on the animal, I noted that the man was wearing a pair of brand name trainers which probably cost more than the repair to my car, and they looked new. His dog did not look underfed either. Fully aware that appearances could be deceptive, I automatically came to the conclusion that begging was a paying game.

As I made for the library car park, I realised I would need a pack of cheap batteries for all the electronic Christmas bits and bobs which might need them. I was about to nip into Poundland again when I noticed that not only were the lights on in Benny's Bargain Basement but the doors were still open. Ordinarily there would be nothing strange about that. Benny kept some of the longest hours of any shopkeeper on the street, opening at eight, and rarely closing before half past six. But Benny was hospitalised, or at least he was the last I heard.

I couldn't help myself. I have to find out what's going on. And anyway, his batteries were as cheap as Poundland's.

The place was an Aladdin's Cave. You could buy almost anything in Benny's and if he didn't have it, he'd get it for you at rock bottom prices. For example as I got older, my knees began to feel the irritation of bending to take a dustpan to the kitchen floor, usually required courtesy Dennis or Cappy the Cat. So I went shopping for one of those long-handled dustpan and brush sets. The prices were outrageous; anything up to eight or nine pounds for two pieces of moulded plastic and some man-made bristles. So I went to Benny's instead, and he didn't have any such thing, but he promised he would get me one within forty-eight hours, and he did. The price? Two pounds ninety-nine. He now carried them as stock but I noticed the price was three ninety-nine. Didn't I tell the keeper of the hospital's secrets that I was one of Benny's best customers?

There was no sign of Benny. Instead it was his son, Barry, working to tidy up the shop, and handle customers at the same time. He did not look exactly overjoyed to see me, but he still managed a weary smile of greeting.

"How's your dad?" I asked.

"He's come round, thanks, Christine. Mam's

with him, and so's Vicky, my missus. He's worn out, though, and he can't remember anything about what happened."

"But he will be home for Christmas?"

"We think so. We're not sure. Concussion, the doctor's reckon. It's a funny thing, isn't it? They're keeping an eye on him and if they let him go tomorrow or Friday, we'll have to watch him, make sure he doesn't slip back." He gave me a tired shrug. "There's nowt I can do at the hospital, and we've lost a day and a half's trade so I thought I'd better open up for the last few hours this afternoon. See what we can salvage." He gestured round at the store. "The coppers made a bigger mess than whoever hit the old man, you know. Flipping fingerprint powder and other gunge here there and everywhere. One or two of the customers have commented on it."

"That's people, Barry. They'll always find something to moan about."

"Oh, they haven't been nasty or nowt. In fact most people are like you. They're really concerned over Dad. And we're grateful for it. You know. He's well-known and well-liked in this town."

"An institution," I agreed. "But he hasn't a clue what happened? Who fired this gunshot or anything?"

"Not a bit. And that's another thing. Everybody says they heard this gunshot, yet the police can't find any trace of weapons being used. They reckon they'd expect to find spent cartridges and places where a bullet or shot had hit the walls or the displays, and in this place—" he waved a loose arm round at the crowded shelves and free-standing displays, "—they might even find gunshot residue, but they were in here all day yesterday and again this morning, and they didn't find anything to suggest a weapon being discharged."

"And Benny doesn't own a gun?"

Barry let loose a sardonic laugh. More of a grunt really. "The police asked me that, and yes, he does have a twelve bore, but it's at home, where it should be. It belonged to my granddad and it hasn't been fired in years."

He moved behind the counter to serve a young couple who had picked up a basket full of Benny's bargains, and I was tempted to leave, but there was something I had to ask. It was delicate and I had an idea what the immediate answer would be, but I needed to ask it, so I ambled round the shop while he dealt with his customers.

Aladdin's Cave, I called it, and the description was apt. I had no idea where Benny did his wholesale buying, but he literally stocked everything, and it wasn't that well organised. I wandered down the far aisle and within the space of a few feet I switched from boxes of chocolates to washing powder to small bales of towels and then woolly gloves. DIY came next, and adjacent to it was a free-standing display of electronic equipment, anything and everything from radio microphones to digital cameras to small, battery powered, megaphones, the kind rappers sometimes used, to a couple of musical keyboards augmented by a range of cheap tablets and smartphones. And as I passed that display – and picked up my requisite pack of batteries – I came to kitchen equipment; plastic bowls and laundry baskets, and the kind of stand-up dustpan and brush I'd prompted him to stock. I turned the corner at the bottom of the shop and hit breakfast cereals right next to dog and cat food, which reminded me that Cappy the Cat would be peckish by the time I got home, so I picked up half a dozen tins, and made for the checkout.

"Is there anything you don't sell, Barry?" I asked as I handed over a couple of pounds.

He chuckled. "If there is, it's only because Dad hasn't thought of it." He handed me my change.

The delicate question came back to the front of my mind. "Barry, is there any danger your dad would talk to me if I visited him?" There. I had asked the question. I hastened on as a frown crossed his brow. "I'm not hassling him and I'm certainly not going to tackle him on what happened, but my viewers will be interested enough to want to hear about his progress."

"I don't know, Christine. All I can say is, ask the nurses. Here, let me give you the ward number."

He scribbled the number out on a piece of paper, I thanked him, tucked it in my purse and walked out into the chilly night… smack into Jack Frogshaw and he didn't appear to be in the best of moods.

He pushed me back against the windows of the bank next door to Benny's. "What did I tell you about minding your own business, keeping your trap shut?"

"As far as I can recall, nothing, but you did shoot your mouth over a lot of other stuff. Now get your hands off me."

Letting me go looked like the last thing he was ready to do.

I was shaking, scared half to death. What made it worse was there were other people around, but none seemed to want to interfere. They obviously thought that Frogshaw and I were man and wife, and our arguments were none of their business. I was appalled at the idea that other people I might think me the kind of woman who would have anything to do with an idiot like Frogshaw, but then, when I was on the force, I had plenty to do with men like him.

I had to remind myself that I was no longer a police officer and that any second now, he would bounce me all over the pavement, and with an armful of shopping, I wasn't really in a position to defend myself.

"You grassed me up, you cow, sent the filth to my door."

"I did nothing of the kind."

"Lying your way out of it won't work either. I'm gonna—"

He never got around to telling me what he was going to do. Before he could specify the threat, a large hand landed on his shoulder, dragged him back and spun him round, and I thanked the lord for my son, the police officer.

Only it wasn't Simon. It was Barry Barnes, and he looked in a worse mood than Frogshaw.

"Picking on a defenceless woman, Froggy? Just about your mark, innit?"

I wasn't sure I liked being described as defenceless, but since Barry appeared to be in control, I chose not to intervene.

To give credit, if that's the right word, Frogshaw didn't immediately back down. "Mind your own business, Barnes."

"I'm making it my business. Y'see, my old man is in dry dock, and according to plod, your boy had a hand in putting him there, and since your bloodnut son isn't here, I can take it out on you, can't I?"

"He had nowt to do with what happened to your old fella."

I couldn't be certain but it sounded like Frogshaw was getting worried. It was probably justified. I'd never taken much notice before, but Barry was a lot taller and beefier than most people realised. It's the kind of thing which was normally hidden behind his white, shopkeeper's smock. If I were Harry Kepler I'd place my bets on Barry.

Barnes the Younger released him. "Come hassling my customers again and next time you'll be in the next bed to my old man. Now sling your hook."

Emboldened by Barry's obvious control of the situation, I chipped in. "Just a minute. No one sent the police to you, Mr Frogshaw. They were looking into the business in Mr Barnes's shop and as I told you, your son was on that video."

"Well it was nowt to do with him." Frogshaw's lips curled but I couldn't work out whether it was fear or contempt. "Get that into your head. My lad had nowt to do with what happened here."

"In that case scram," Barry said, "and don't you come threatening my customers again."

Frogshaw skulked away and I beamed upon my

hero. "Thank you, Barry."

"No problem, Christine. I…"

He trailed off as Patience Shuttle hobbled to us. "Seen him off good and proper, have you, young Barry? Aye, well, it's time someone did."

"Eaten bigger for breakfast, Ms Shuttle," Barry replied.

"So what did he want?" Patience asked.

"He thought I told the police about his son being here during yesterday morning's disturbance, Patience," I replied. "He was wrong. I think his son was here yesterday, but that's not to say he had a hand in what happened."

"Wouldn't surprise anyone if he did, though, would it? Well, better get on."

Patience shuffled along and I concentrated on Barry again. "As a matter of interest, Barry, how did you hear about young Frogshaw? I thought your dad couldn't speak."

"Mandy Hiscoe. She was at the hospital yesterday, and she told us one of the kids running away looked like Froggy's lad."

"Ah. Right. Well, I'd better do like Patience and get off home. Thanks again for looking after me, Barry. I hope your dad's on the mend real soon."

Chapter Eleven

It was getting on for half past six when I finally pulled into the drive, and learned, much to my astonishment, that Dennis was already home. His car was not there, so I didn't truly realise it until I walked into the kitchen and found him rooting through the freezer. This was simply baffling. He never got home before seven, and sometimes it was getting on for eight before I saw him.

"What happened?" I asked as I walked into the kitchen. "Did someone cut the electricity off at Haxford Fixers or has the building burned down?"

"Ha-flipping-ha. Me and Geronimo went out to Ivy Saperia's place to fit her kitchen cabinet doors, and I got Geronimo to drop me off. He'll pick me up at half past seven tomorrow morning. Anyway, never mind me, where've you been?"

"In the wars. I'll tell you later. For now, what are you looking for in the freezer? A slice of gravy?"

This catty remark did little to improve his mood. "That's the trouble with you. You think I'm a numpty in the kitchen. I know for a fact you keep gravy in the top cupboard. I was looking for some chips."

I instructed him to make us both a cup of tea, and then shooed him out of the kitchen while I took off my coat and set about getting something quick and simple. With his search in mind, I dug out a bag of oven chips and to go with them, I chose breaded cod and the last of the can of peas which were open from the previous day. Tea under way, I emptied my shopping bags, moved to the living room where I booted up the laptop on the workstation and left the memory stick to one side. Like it or not, I would have to work through the evening.

When I told Dennis, it was like I'd just told him I'd won the lottery.

"Good," he said. "Bullit's on the telly and I can watch that. I love that car chase."

Why else would he watch it, I asked myself as work in the kitchen and Cappy the Cat's pleas for food began to pile the pressure on.

"Dennis, will you put some food down for this cat?"

"I don't see why I should," he grumbled as he came into the kitchen. "He never feeds me."

"No, but he does help by clearing up the crumbs you leave on the carpet."

"A blinking gannet. That's what he is. Eat anything."

By mutual agreement, Dennis and Cappy the Cat had little to do with one another. The cat never liked Dennis, and while my husband could take or leave cats, he was really a dog man.

"I grew up with dogs," you could hear him say regularly, and it was true. Back in the days when he and I were first dating, I'd call at his house to be greeted by a crazy Boxer aptly named Nutter on account of his habit of head-butting everything when he was excited. And I do mean everything: doors, walls, dustbins, people, everything. He went the way of all crackpot dogs when he head butted a moving car and it won. By that time, Dennis's love of engines had become an obsession and while his brothers and sisters were distressed by Nutter's demise, Dennis took it in his stride. "You can't expect to drop the nut on a Mark Two Cortina and come away with nowt but a headache," he said with a philosophical air I never before suspected in him.

A little over an hour later, with the meal over, the pots and dishes in the dishwasher, Cappy the Cat snoozing in his basket, Dennis homing in on the TV, I settled down at my workstation to begin work.

First I fished out my spy camera to see what it might have picked up, but when I plugged it in, the battery was dead. In the flurry of the afternoon's activity, I'd forgotten to switch it off, and the rotten little thing wasn't designed to charge from a USB connection. Without the adaptor, I had no means of charging it, and I came to the reluctant conclusion that Kim was right when she said my IT equipment was out of date. I also came to the second conclusion that Dennis was half right about the adaptor situation. I needed a new one and so close to Christmas, Lester Grimes's offer of a replacement looked like the best solution. Even if I found what I was looking for on the web, I wouldn't see it until the end of the following week, and I needed it ASAP.

I've never approved of breaking the law, and Dennis's earlier announcement, 'you won't get a guarantee with it', coupled with my solid knowledge of Lester Grimes was enough to tell me that it was stolen. Not that Lester would have stolen it, but he'd never been too choosy about where he secured his spares, and as long as the price was right, which in this case probably meant a pound, or at the most, two he wouldn't ask any questions concerning its pedigree. Chances were that he bought it from a friend of a friend who knew a man who knew where to get his hands on one.

Reluctant though I was to take it, I needed it so I broke into Dennis's study of a repeat of Top Gear, and told him to pick the adaptor up for me tomorrow, and I received a grunt by return. I knew he would need a more forcible reminder.

After that, I tracked down and paid for the genuine article (at a cost of £15) from an online supplier, but as I suspected, they couldn't deliver until after New Year. I gave Dennis a reminder of Lester's offer and got another grunt back. Whenever Dennis was engrossed in something on the television or a magazine article (mechanics-style magazines, naturally) it caused me to wonder why we humans ever bothered developing language.

With no other distractions to, er, distract me, I inserted the memory stick Kim had given me, and opened up the menu. Because of its size, the afternoon's video was easy to pick out from the half dozen files on the stick. The others were also videos but they bore cryptic titles like BDANDV, HSMD, and MADA. I was intrigued to know what they were, but I didn't have time. I had an entire afternoon's security footage to get through.

Like Tuesday's it was tedious in the extreme. Even at 16x speed I found myself yawning, and the only time I slowed it to normal speed, or drifted back and reran scenes was when someone took an interest in Medical/Biochemistry. It wasn't often. Rita Nuffield spent a minute or two there, and I anticipated seeing Kepler, too, until I remembered he was barred. Patience Shuttle, who seemed to be as frequent a visitor to the library as Kepler, Rita and co. appeared, but Patience was interested in the general science section facing Medical/Biochemistry. She took down a book and then sat at the reading table with her back to the camera, and for a moment, I wondered... but it wasn't theft from General Science we were looking into, and anyway she put the book back after a few minutes. Heaven alone knew what she was doing in that section, but I remembered she'd been scanning that same shelf the day before. It seemed wholly incongruous for a woman of her advanced years, but perhaps she was taking an OU degree. Well, it wasn't entirely unknown for old dears like her, was it?

Aside from those two oases of brief interest, I barely recognised any of the other transient visitors to that little enclave, and an hour after starting work, I could feel my eyelids drooping.

It did occur to me that the Religion and Philosophy section was not covered by our camera, and for the life of me, I couldn't work out where it was in the library. I would need a second camera; mine.

For the third time I spoke to the old man. "Did

you ring Lester?"

Grunt.

I stomped round to the front of the settee, snatched up the TV remote and for a moment, I was tempted to switch if off, but that would be grossly unfair. I knew how I would react if Dennis did that to me. Instead I paused the picture.

"Hey. I was watching that."

"And I'm talking to you. It's a smart TV, Dennis. You can freeze the picture whenever you want and play catch up. At a pinch, you can even record it. Now have you rung Lester Grimes?"

His brow knitted. "Why would I wanna ring Grimy?"

Having suffered an afternoon of raw stress, my patience was wafer thin. "The adaptor for my little camera. You said he could get me one for five pounds."

"Oh that?" He took the TV remote back. "It's in me work bag."

"You never said anything when I got in."

"I forgot, didn't I? And, hey, while I think on, you owe me a fiver."

"With a memory like yours, remind me in the morning."

But Dennis had already gone back to whatever he was watching.

I slipped my shoes on and drew a cardigan over my back to combat the cold and nipped outside and into the garage where he kept his overalls, spare tools, gardening equipment, the lawnmower, and where he left his canvas workbag every night. It was a throwback, a habit which stemmed from the days when he worked at Addison's, days when he would take a flask and sandwiches to work. Like his partners, he was a regular at Sandra's Snacky so he carried nothing in it these days apart from what he considered essentials. I was hard pressed to work out what was essential about a dog-eared paperback copy of Ian Fleming's *Moonraker*. In over thirty years, I'd never known Dennis Capper read anything other than the Haynes Manuals for the various vehicles he worked on. He didn't even buy newspapers. I'd never read the book in question, but I was willing to bet that Mr Fleming had described some classic motor car down to the last nut and bolt.

In amongst a couple of tatty copies of Classic Motoring, a stack of receipts which I had no doubt would be dumped on me when it came to doing his books, I found the adaptor, and hurried out, locked the garage and rushed back inside out of the cold.

Like so many things to do with Dennis (his precious car excepted) the thing was covered in oil or grease, and I had to scrub both it and my hands clean before I could examine it properly. It looked like mine, it had a similar rating to mine (from what I could remember) but it was not made by the same company, so it was with some trepidation that I took it back to the workstation, plugged it into a multi-socket board and hooked my camera into it. Lo and behold, it worked. Or should I say, the red light, which indicated the camera picking up a charge, came on?

On past experience, it would take anything up to two hours before it was fully charged, so I was left with two options; sit there twiddling my thumbs or watch another repeat of Top Gear before Dennis tuned in to his feature film.

I returned to the kitchen, unloaded the dishwasher and switched on the kettle.

"If you're making some tea, I'll have one," Dennis called from the living room.

His selective deafness never ceased to amaze me. I spoke to him three times about Lester's procurement of an adaptor and he didn't hear. Yet he heard me press the switch on the kettle while he was in a different room, and ours was not the noisiest kettle switch in Christendom.

Feeling skittish, I called back, "The kettle doesn't have my name on it, you know."

"Russell Hobbs if I remember right."

I was rapidly losing control of a) the evening and b) my temper. I made tea, trooped back into the living room, plonked a cup down in front of him while he leaned over to look round me and at the TV screen. Getting seriously wound up, I returned to the workstation, and stared at the memory stick Kim had passed to me. There were those other files on it which I hadn't looked at. If the memory stick belonged to Upley, they were probably videos of the annual general meeting of the Haxford Pickety-Nickety Society. That was unfair considering Upley's present state of grief, but it was an adequate summary of the man.

I slotted the stick into a USB port and opened the first file.

It was a meeting all right, but nothing to do with any Haxford society I'd ever come across.

Complete with sound, it was a meeting between a young woman and two men, all significantly lacking in clothing, and there were only certain of parts of them involved in the meeting.

The most shocking aspect of this was the realisation that the memory stick and its content must belong to Alden Upley. He could not have confiscated it because no one could have been watching it in the library. Their computer terminals were fitted with USB ports but everyone would see what you were watching. And even if someone had the sheer neck to watch the video, Upley did not have the authority to confiscate anything. He could ask them to remove it, certainly, he could demand that they leave the premises, but he had no authority to relieve them of the offending material. Logically, therefore, it had to be his, and that made me even more annoyed. It was no business of mine or anyone else's how Alden Upley got his jollies, but set this alongside his officious, bumptious, holier-than-thou attitude, and it spelled hypocrisy on a scale not seen since the last general election.

As a police officer, I'd come across hard core pornography any number of times and it didn't so much disgust as annoy me. How on earth could anyone, male or female, sink to such a level that they were willing to appear on camera doing what comes naturally but what should be done in privacy. The arguments against me were all economic – i.e. they got paid to do it – and that only made matters worse in my book.

"What in the name of Whitworth spanners and ABS magnets are you watching?"

I was so lost in my ruminations that I didn't realise Dennis had overheard the fake moans and groans and came round to see what the fuss was about. I stopped the video immediately and removed the memory stick

His attitude to such videos was similar to mine. He was all in favour of a total ban on hard-core pornography, which sounded seriously strait-laced and political until you learned that his idea of pornography was watching someone using a power saw to cut up the bodywork of a Hillman Avenger for scrap, or worse, taking an adjustable spanner to nuts and bolts instead of the correct size of proper spanners. When it comes to the genuine article, such as Alden Upley's preference, he was exactly like me. Not interested. He didn't even keep men's magazines at the workshop.

It's a long time ago, but I recall the first time I ever talked to him about libido and with hindsight I should have guessed his response.

"I suppose that's the latest piece of junk from Fiat, is it? The Libido."

I remember thinking at the time that it had a certain ring to it. 'Oh, I've just bought a brand new Fiat Libido, you know.'

Dennis was half a year younger than me, and at our time of life, the issue didn't trouble us as often as it used to but that didn't mean we were dead from the waist down. I recalled an incident when daughter Ingrid was about sixteen years old and came home one evening and caught us, er, in flagrante. She was thoroughly disgusted. "Don't you think you're a bit old for that kind of stuff?"

she yelled before hurrying out of the room.

Well, no, quite frankly, we were not too old, and it was with no little surprise that I realised the few seconds of the video I had watched had had a slight effect on me. I turned to face him, a slow-burning smile on my lips.

Dennis understood at once. "Aw, come on, Chrissy, I've gotta be up for work and Geronimo's coming to pick me up, and I wanted to watch Bullit."

"Record it," I ordered him, "and fire a few bullets in my direction."

I often heard other women complaining about husbands demanding a bit too much... you know. In our house, it was the other way round. Not that I demanded too much but long as Dennis's idea of hedonism was a Sunday morning romp round the scrap yards, seeing what bits and pieces he could find, it was always left to me to take the lead.

Later, as we drifted off to the bedroom, I knew Dennis would sleep well, dreaming of 1967 Vauxhall Vivas, and he would go off to work tomorrow grumbling about backache and my unreasonable demands upon him, but it would leave me in a different frame of mind, one that was ready to take on half a dozen Jack Frogshaws, two dozen Graveyard Poisoners and Alden Upley... especially Alden Upley.

Chapter Twelve

Dennis was still grumbling about his bad back and having missed one of his favourite films when Tony Wharrier called for him a couple of minutes after half past seven on Thursday morning. I had work I needed to get through before I left for the library, so for once, I was up as he left the house, and he warned me, "I'll be late tonight, Chrissy. I have to call to see me mam."

This was not just unusual, it was almost unheard of. Eunice Capper was pushing eighty and lived in sheltered accommodation the other side of Haxford. It was when she got to that stage where she needed not exactly looking after, but someone on call nearby, that I invited her to come and live with us. Dennis didn't want it, I didn't want it, but I felt it only right to make the offer because I got on all right with the old girl and now that Simon and Ingrid had flown the coop, we had room. I needn't have worried. Eunice didn't want it either. All her friends lived in the same, sheltered housing development and she'd rather be with them.

And Dennis was visiting her? Why?

One look at the calendar reminded me. December 23rd was Eunice's birthday. She was (I think) seventy-nine years old. I was horrified with myself. How could I have forgotten? I was the one in this house who remembered birthdays, not Dennis. We'd already paid our annual Christmas visit a week or two back, and taken her a bottle of her favourite brandy, a Christmas card and birthday card, but I knew I had to ring her today, just to wish her a happy birthday. It was an annual ritual, and I should have known. If that was the effect a short-lived, under the duvet encounter had on my memory, perhaps it was time to take Ingrid's ill meant irritation more seriously.

Putting it all to the back of my mind, I toyed with a bowl of Shredded Wheat while I considered the day ahead.

I would have to ring the hospital to check on Benny Barnes's situation, see if I could get a word with him. So much of that little mystery remained unsolved. I had no clue where to go on the Graveyard Poisoner or the murder of Evelyn Upley, and precious little to report on the book thief, but I did need a word with Alden Upley. More than a word.

It would be difficult. Newly widowed, his grief at a peak, I would have to handle the situation delicately, tactfully, and I didn't really see it as my place to lecture anyone on their, er, viewing habits. If Kim's analysis of the Upley marriage was anything to go by, however, perhaps Alden felt it necessary, but he needed to take a little care about where he left the evidence lying around. Either that or he should learn to lock his desk when he wasn't in the staff room.

Grieving or not, he would have to be told.

There was another angle to this. Working as a private investigator wasn't all plain sailing. There were times when it could be difficult getting information out of people, and I never knew when I might need a bit of leverage... when he got over Evelyn's death, naturally. Call it blackmail if you wish. I prefer the term persuasion. On my life, I would never go running to his wife with what I knew (I couldn't now, could I?) and I would certainly never use it on my vlog, but Upley didn't need to know that, did he?

I had to be at the library for dead on nine o'clock if I was to catch Alden on his own, which was the reason I got out of bed so early, but before I could go anywhere, I wanted to check the footage from my camera (if there was any) to see what, if anything, it wanted to tell me before it ran out of steam.

Lester's adaptor, for which Dennis still had not got back his fiver because he forgot to ask me for it, did a proper job on the camera, and when I hooked it into my laptop, I learned that not only was it fully charged, but the camera held almost four hours of video footage. I was under the impression that when the battery died, it would automatically wipe the memory, because that's what always happened with my compact digital camera. I forgot, however, that I was storing the footage on a mini SD card, which meant it kept the recording up to and including the mains cable being ripped out – two and a half hours – and for a further ninety minutes beyond that. Right up to the moment when the camera's internal power source gave out.

The first two and a half hours were the same as all the other footage. Boring and uneventful. A few people looked at the Medical/Biochemistry shelf, amongst them Patience Shuttle, who soon turned her attention to General Science. The footage only became interesting when Harry Kepler interfered with the camera, and despite what I was told, interfered was the correct word.

To listen to Upley and Kim's explanation, it sounded as if Kepler spotted the camera, wondered what it was, yanked it down and the books falling from the shelves broke the cable, but it was nothing of the kind. He didn't even appear on the video until he climbed on the lower shelves, and even then it was only the top of his head and his evil eye which were caught on screen. He looked into the lens, and then turned his head to follow the line of the cable as it ran along the top of the rack to the wall. Up to that point, Kim and Upley could have been telling the truth. What happened next threw it all out of court. Kepler prised the camera from the shelf, and uprooted the Sellotape close by. But when he couldn't reach any further, he climbed down and the picture began to go haywire.

First it was a wonderful view of his filthy palm holding the camera, then the camera was swinging free, as he attended to the cable further up and at one point, his hand disappeared into his pocket from where he withdrew a small clasp knife and hacked through the mains cable as far as he could. That done, he dropped the knife back in his pocket and broke the cable at that point, and he must have dropped the camera in his pocket, too, because the picture all but blacked out. I could still hear, though, and he was obviously climbing on the shelf again and tearing the cable away from its Sellotape. That went on for a few seconds before I heard the clatter of books falling from the shelf. I guessed he must have pulled too hard and set the entire rack rocking. Then I heard Upley's voice and the jumble of movement as Kepler got off the shelf.

Throughout the only words I heard clearly were Upley's when he demanded. "What's that dangling from your pocket?"

Kepler gave him a couple of coarse rejoinders, perhaps predictable with hindsight, before the camera emerged once more into the light, but it was looking straight up at the ceiling. More argument followed, and although the sound wasn't too good, I was sure I heard Kepler say someone had told him about the camera and it was an invasion of privacy. Then Upley banned him from the library and took the camera from him. At length, after even more argument, Kepler left the building delivering a tirade of Anglo-Saxon and Upley returned to the counter, where he examined the camera close up.

It was unnerving staring into his giant eye and then up his right nostril before he tucked it away, safe under the counter where it remained until I collected it, but between then and getting home, the battery had run out of steam.

I would never describe myself as bad-tempered. Outspoken when I had to be, determined when necessary, but not a snapper. At that moment, however, I was furious, absolutely livid with three people; Upley, Kim and Harry Kepler, and of the three, the librarian and his assistant were the worst miscreants. Kepler sabotaged that camera deliberately, probably because he was going to steal it, but Upley and Kim tried to pass it off as some kind accident, the result of Kepler's inquisitiveness. Yet Upley caught him in the act. He knew what Kepler was about, but he tried to flannel me. And Kim backed him. We were friends, Kim and me. I'd known her since well, forever, and this is what she did to me? What kind of betrayal was that? Why couldn't people take a leaf from Dennis's book and tell it like it was? He might not be the most exciting man in the world to live with, he might be too laid back, he might be mechanically obsessed, but he was honest and open.

I was seething as I shoved a hungry Cappy the Cat out of my way. He hissed back at me, I ignored him and checked the clock, an action which aside from telling me it was a quarter to nine, also added to my anger. Not the time but the instrument's lack of tinsel. Didn't I buy the fizzing stuff yesterday?

I had intended to speak quietly and sympathetically to Upley about his interest in films carnal, but the mood I was in, I didn't care who heard about it, and since I was just as annoyed with Kim, she would get an earful too.

I snatched my coat and was about to storm out of the house when Cappy the Cat pestered me again, pawing me, sitting at my feet and casting a hypnotic stare up at me. "What do you want, you feline…"

The begging eyes brought me up short. He hadn't been fed. Left to Dennis, Cappy the Cat would not be fed until the poor mite was fainting through malnutrition. Not that he was cruel – Dennis, I mean, not Cappy the Cat. He just lived in a different world to the rest of us. And he wouldn't have thought to let Cappy the Cat out, either.

I hung my coat back on the hook and made for the kitchen, where I opened the back door. While Cappy the Cat shot out into the garden, I opened a packet of his food and dropped it in his dish then refreshed his water. By the time it was ready he was back in and heading for the bowl. I left him tucking into the food.

Wrapped up against the shocking weather, my temper had cooled, largely thanks to Cappy the Cat. I drove sedately down to town, round the back of the library and parked up. I spent a few moments rehearsing my approach, and climbed out just as Patience Shuttle's ancient van pulled into the car park and both Kepler and Rita Nuffield climbed out with her.

"I gave them a lift," Patience explained to me as they wandered off towards the High Street. "I was on my way to the library anyway."

"You're quite a voracious reader, aren't you, Patience?" I commented as we fell in side by side for the short walk to the library front door.

"You'll know when you get to my age, Christine. Nowt better to do than stare at the four walls, and there's never nowt on telly is there?"

"I don't disapprove," I reassured her. "I like nothing better than to curl up with a good book." Could I? Dare I? How could I without giving away the secret surveillance. "My friend, Kim, was telling me how you're taking an interest in scientific matters."

"You mean you saw me on your spy camera thing?"

So much for secrecy. Was it MI5 or MI6? One of them dealt with foreign spies, the other dealt with homemade spies. Whichever way round it was, I guessed they wouldn't be too enthusiastic should I decide to apply for a position as a modern Mata Hari.

"There are things going on in the library, Patience, and Mr Upley has asked me to look into them. Please don't spread it around."

"No problem, lass, but if you want to keep it secret, you could do better than asking your husband to realign the cameras. I'm not saying your Dennis is a bigmouth, but he's not exactly the most discreet bloke in Haxford, is he?"

Neither are his two partners. Once again, I didn't verbalise my immediate thought. "So what particular science are you looking into?" I asked. Anything to avoid a discussion on Dennis and his pals.

"Agronomy. It's all about producing better plants and crops. I thought it might help with the garden, but it's all way above me." Patience chuckled. "Shows you what a daft old so and so I can be, don't it?" She paused at the door. "You're not taking the library over then?"

The question stumped me for a moment. "Whatever gave you such an idea?"

"You did. T'other day, you said you were here on business and when I asked whether you were thinking of getting rid of Alden you said it never entered your head to sack him."

"Oh, I was only joking."

I said it with a smile, but the light-heartedness skipped over Patience's head. "Good. He's a fine man, Alden Upley, and he has such a sad life that the library is all he's got. Although I reckon he's better off now than he were yesterday."

I put aside her blatant disregard for Evelyn Upley's life. She had such a high opinion of Upley that she couldn't know about his collection of home movies, could she? "A sad life?"

"That wife of his. Evelyn. I told you, didn't I, if you had a cat as bad as her, you'd strangle the flaming thing. A spiteful, vicious, vindictive old bat, she was. He always deserved better."

Patience's opinion fitted with Kim's as voiced in the Tavern the previous evening, and if Mrs Upley really was that kind of virago, it might explain his interest in videos depicting close encounters of the salacious kind.

All of which had little or nothing to do with my visit to the library. I held the door open for Patience and followed her in.

The doors had only opened a few minutes earlier, and the barflies were already in residence, while at the counter, both Upley and Kim were busy dealing with returned books. There were a few browsers checking out the different shelves, but no one looking at Medical/Biochemistry. A casual glance up at the security camera above and adjacent to the portioned off reading room indicated it was still looking in the right direction. Why wouldn't it be?

Kim acknowledged me with a thin smile, Upley,

pale-faced, lacking any sign of sparkle, invited me to go to the staff room and make myself a cup of tea until he could join me.

The conversation with Patience and the tea helped further cool my irritation and by the time Kim floated off to replace books in their official repository, and Upley joined me, I was brisk rather than brusque, and yet oozing sympathy.

"You have news for us, Mrs Capper?"

"Not as such. Never mind the stolen books, Alden. How are you?"

He took his time answering, and I thought he would burst into tears. "As well as one might expect given the circumstances."

"Yes. Of course. Please accept my condolences." After a momentary pause, I dug out and held up the incriminating memory stick. "I'm simply returning this. There were a couple of items which came out of yesterday's recordings which I need to discuss with you, and the first is this memory stick."

His ears had coloured on sight of the memory stick. "Ah. Oh. I, er…"

He trailed off and I took the initiative. "In respect of your situation, Alden, Kim broke a few rules yesterday afternoon, but I didn't leave her much choice. She copied yesterday's footage onto this. Kim didn't look at the other videos stored on it. I did." I paused a moment and watched his cheeks turn crimson. "It's not my place to tell you what you should and shouldn't be watching, but I would strongly advise you not to keep this kind of thing lying around here where anyone might pick it up. If you must view it on the premises, at least keep it in your pocket, or at the very worst, lock it away somewhere. In fact, come to think, it might be better if you locked the content with a password."

He took the stick from me, dropped it in his pocket and with a sigh, sat down. "I was remiss, and please accept my apologies." He was silent for a moment and I guessed there was more to come. He swallowed a large lump in his throat. "Evelyn – my wife – you see. We've been married many, many years, and I love her dearly, but she doesn't appreciate that a man has needs." I noticed he was still talking about her in the present tense.

"So do women."

"Yes, yes. I understand that, but it doesn't appear to apply to Mrs Upley."

This time he did break down and cry and it took some minutes to calm him down. I felt like a complete dragon, every bit as bad as his late wife.

When he dried his tears, he was almost pleading. "I'm not old, Christine."

That was unusual. I'd always known Alden Upley as the epitome of formality. He even addressed Kim, a woman he'd worked with for many years, as Ms Aspinall, and hadn't he just referred to his wife as 'Mrs Upley'? According to my memory, he had never addressed me by my given name.

Every word was interspersed with the effort to catch his breath. "I'm not over the hill, but Evelyn doesn't – didn't see it in quite the same way. She doesn't – didn't understand the sheer... er... the sheer frustration, the pressure."

It was not a discussion I was prepared to get into.

"I said, it's not my place to judge you, Alden, but please be careful where you leave such things lying around."

"I will, and again, please accept my apologies." He appeared relieved when he changed the subject. "You said there were issues arising from yesterday's recording."

"One issue. And it didn't come from your camera but mine. When Kepler ripped down my camera, he didn't realise it was still running. What you tried to pass off as an accident was a deliberate act on his part. He was trying to steal the camera. You caught him red-handed."

He blushed again. "Yes. I did."

"Yet you didn't think to tell me the truth."

"Well, I..."

It occurred to me that we weren't making much progress, which was perhaps understandable, but when he trailed off, his eyes shifted to the staff room door where Kim stood.

"That was my fault, Chrissy," she admitted.

I swivelled round to look at her. "Why?"

"I thought you had enough on your plate trying to catch our thief, and we'd like it cleared up before Christmas, if possible. Then you're shoving your oar into the business at Benny's. I figured you could do without that little scroat, Kepler, distracting you. I mean, it's not like you're ever going to sue him for the cost of the damage, is it? Well, you might, but let's face it, you won't have a snowball in hell's chance of getting your money back."

"You're probably right, but there are other issues at stake, principally honesty, by which I mean you being honest with me. You've hired me to do a job and the least you can do is be absolutely candid with me."

Kim shrugged. "Sorry."

"And again, I apologise," Alden added.

"Right. In that case, we'll say no more about it. I dug into my bag again and came out with the cube camera and the new mains adaptor. "I've replaced the damaged parts, and if you're amenable, I can set up again. Kim tells me you've had another book stolen."

By now, apparently content to talk business, Upley was more in control of himself. "Hardly relevant, I feel, Mrs Capper. This was from the social, religious, philosophy and theology section, a marked divergence from our thief's usual line of interest."

I had my doubts about that and spelled them out. "One of the thief's previous prizes was something to do with embalming. That goes hand in hand with funeral services. It's no problem for me to…"

A chuckle from Kim, still stood by the door where she could keep her eye on the counter, interrupted me.

"It's probably the Graveyard Poisoner," she said, and my blood ran cold.

"Oh, my dear God, you're right. That's exactly who it is."

Chapter Thirteen

"Run that by me again," Paddy Quinn demanded.

I knew when we called the police that this would be his attitude. Detective Inspector Patrick Quinn had an irritating habit of disregarding anyone who came up with ideas he and his team had not thought of.

An inch or two short of six feet, his hair thinning, he was smartly dressed (weren't all CID officers) but his dark tie was pulled down at the collar to ensure he gave out that impression of a harassed detective. I guessed he must be getting on for sixty and probably had one eye on early retirement once he got there. He'd been a police officer forever, and in truth he was an excellent detective. That was one of the hallmarks of your common or garden Haxforder. They tended get into a job and no matter how many different employers they worked for, they stuck at it and they were the best, even if that job only entailed sweeping the streets. So Paddy was good, but he was a major pain in the BTM in that he had this air of disbelief about him. He assumed that everyone he spoke to was either lying or fantasising.

When the realisation dawned on me, at Kim's prompt, it gave rise to another bout of annoyance and self-recrimination. Alden gave me the list of stolen books on Tuesday but I paid scant attention to it. I was too busy looking into the business at Benny's – which was really none of my concern – and working through the tedious downloads from the cameras. With hindsight, I should have made the connection when I was checking into the history of the Graveyard Poisoner's victims, but I did not, and yet, Alden's list was right there in front of me on my workstation.

I was convinced of the connection, and Mandy, who turned up with him, was... let's say interested, but with Quinn clearly ready to dismiss it, I had to draw in a breath and mentally count to three. "It's simple enough, Mr Quinn. We, that is Mr Upley, Ms Aspinall and I, believe the Graveyard Poisoner is stealing books from the library in an effort to get his technique right."

Quinn picked up the list of books. "And you're basing that assumption on the titles of these knocked off books? You know, you were a good copper, Chrissy, but all these years of sitting at home twiddling your thumbs has addled your brain."

Alongside him, Mandy only just managed to suppress her cringe. She probably guessed what was coming... from me.

And she was right. I could feel my anger rising again. "And too many hours of watching foolish American cops and robbers movies has led you along a silly path where everything is kill or be killed." He tried to interrupt but I talked right over him. "Look at the list again, and assume, just for one moment, that this is the work of one person. Even if he turns out not to be the Graveyard Poisoner, you're still looking at a man with a disturbed mind."

While we were waiting for them to arrive, Upley, Kim and I drew up a full list of the stolen books, and I borrowed a highlighter to pick out the most important titles, those that backed our assumption: *Forensic Techniques in Crime Detection, Embalming: Good Practice, Toxicity of Common Household Chemicals, The Big Book of Funeral Services.* It was with some irritation that I realised the theft of *A Compendium of Funeral Practices* from the previous day was not the first from that section of the library and it married perfectly with the theft of *The Big Book of Funeral Services.*

Still Quinn did not want to listen to me. "For all you know, this might be a history or science student boning up for his exams."

"And for all I know, you might well be a sensible detective, but working on your principles, I shouldn't assume that without evidence."

He returned a look of thunder. "I'll pretend I didn't hear that." He got to his feet. "Take a statement, Mandy… about the stolen books, not the Graveyard Poisoner. When you've done that, get back to the station. If you don't find me in the office, I'll be in the canteen."

We all four watched him tromp out of the staff room. Kim followed him, to man the counter, and Mandy wagged a disapproving finger at me.

"You shouldn't wind him up like that, Chrissy. I have to work with him."

"Then he should improve his people skills. Alden, Kim and I discussed this before ringing you, and although I'm fully convinced, I can't prove it. We were doing our civic duty, but Paddy sees it as an annoyance."

"I know, and you do have a point, and I will at least look into it, but to be fair to the boss, it is stretching credibility." As an indication that the debate was over, she turned to Alden. "Right, Mr Upley, can I take it you're authorised to speak on behalf of Haxford Borough Council?"

"I run the library, Ms Hiscoe. I am therefore fully authorised to brief you on the thefts and steps we have taken to identify the culprit, steps which, I might add, are in line with instructions I received from the town hall."

I left them to it, and moved out into the library where I had Kim direct me to the Religion and Philosophy section, and borrowed her wheelie stepladder.

The particular section was tucked away in the far corner of the room, opposite the reading room partition, and there was no convenient power point, but there was one close to the floor tucked up against the reading room partition, presumably located there for the early morning cleaners. Attaching fresh, double-sided tape to the camera base, I climbed the ladder and placed the cube on the very top of the wood and glass partition, and allowed my new cable to run down to the floor socket. News of Harry Kepler's attempt to steal the camera and his subsequent ban from the library would have spread through most of the town never mind the library, and I was confident no one would dare disturb the camera a second time. Aside from anything else, it was now situated about nine feet from the floor and there were no lower shelves for a would-be thief to climb on.

Satisfied, I returned to the staff room to check it on my laptop, but before I could boot up the machine, Mandy cornered me.

"Alden tells me you set up a camera to watch the section where the books were being taken."

"Yes. I've just set it up again after Harry Kepler tore it down. It's above board. The library has signs warning users of security cameras."

"Yes, I know that, but according to Alden, you set up a mini spy-type camera, and they don't just record video, but audio too, and without the permission of those you're recording, that, Chrissy, is illegal."

I shrugged. "I know that, but what can I do? Listen to me, please, Mandy. I'm not interested in conversations, arguments, sounds of any description, but the library needs to stop these thefts. Whoever the culprit, he's not nicking cheap paperbacks. These are expensive hardcovers and he needs to be stopped, and if he really is the Graveyard Poisoner…" I left the suggestion hanging in the air.

"That kind of evidence would be inadmissible precisely because it was illegally procured." She chewed her lip for a moment. "I should order you to stop it now. In fact, I should report you for it."

"Television companies do it, don't they?" I protested. "You know, the old hidden cameras in handbags and stuff. I've seen it."

"I know they do, but that doesn't make it legal." She considered her plight for a moment. "Can you run the camera without audio?"

I shrugged. "Ask me another."

"Do you have any editing software on your laptop?"

I shrugged. "Ask me another."

I could see the exasperation was beginning to get the better of her. "You're running this stuff and you don't know the first thing about it, do you?"

At last, a question I could answer. "I haven't the faintest idea."

"Then learn. All I'm asking, Chrissy is that you dump the audio. If you don't know how to do it, ask someone who does. Your Simon's not bad with computers. Try him. Because, listen to me because I'm telling you, if Paddy finds out about this, he'll book you."

I gave way. "I promise. Now what are you gonna do about the possibility that our book thief is the Graveyard Poisoner?"

"Nothing, at least not until you come up with a suspect. But I'm not Paddy Quinn. Give me your book thief, and I will take it a bit more seriously."

And how was I supposed to come up with a suspect until he struck at the library again, which might well be never.

That's what I was thinking, but I didn't say it.

I'd had enough of arguing, but as I left the library the same thought was swirling round my head. If I was right and the book thief was also the Graveyard Poisoner, then for all we knew he might have already taken enough books for his campaign of murder, and if that was the case, I would never be able to demonstrate the link, which in turn meant Paddy Quinn's estimate of me, already somewhere down near the correct level for crushing underfoot, would sink even lower, all the way into the gutter, and he'd be ready to hose the gutter down and swill me into the sewers.

At that moment, standing on the pavement outside the library, it occurred to me just how sad an excuse for a private investigator I was. I had three enquiries on the go, and I was making no progress on any of them, and I had no idea where to find any information to move them on. All right, so two of them were unofficial, but even on the library book thief, I was doing nothing. I felt like giving it all up and going back to being humble Christine Capper, blogger/vlogger.

Mandy came scurrying past me. "Sorry, Chrissy, gotta dash," she said and rushed round the corner of the building in the direction of the car park. A few moments later she tore past and up Yorkshire Street, headlights blazing, blue lights flashing and I was tempted to follow her, see what was going on, but I changed my mind. I was an investigative washout and whatever it was, I couldn't do it justice.

Like anyone else, I had my share of failings, but self-pity, feeling sorry for myself, wasn't one of them, but right at that moment, I needed some comfort, and where better to find it than Terry's Tea Bar. One of his toasted teacakes and a welcome cup of tea would put the world to rights, or at least, that part of the world I was concerned with.

"Me dad says you wanted a word."

The voice belonged to John Frogshaw who had sneaked up and startled me while I was daydreaming of tea and toasted teacakes. "Oh. Hello, John. You made me jump."

He shrugged. "Me dad reckons I'm better off talking to you than plod."

"He's right. Come on. Fancy a cup of tea?"

"I'd rather have cola."

I led him up Yorkshire Street, into Market Street, into the market hall, where I grabbed a table in Terry's and ordered tea for me, cola for him. I skipped the toasted teacake because it might have obliged me to feed him and by the look of his father's car from yesterday, Jack Frogshaw should be feeding him.

I didn't know John well. I knew of him, of course. All of Haxford knew of the Frogshaws, but that was as far as it went with me. I guessed him to be about sixteen or seventeen years old, tall, rangy, really nondescript, but that shaggy mop of red hair would give him away in a football crowd. When he spoke, it was without the inherent threat in his father's words, and it gave me some kind of faint hope for the future. Maybe the next generation of Frogshaws would be more amenable to their neighbours, more legitimate in their business activities.

"Benny's Bargain Basement," I said, taking a sip from my tea. "Have the police spoken to you?"

"No. They haven't caught up with me yet." Suddenly, without warning there was a plea on his face and in his voice. "It weren't us, missus. We didn't do nowt. We were just larking about and we legged it when Benny hassled us."

"Slow down, slow down," I urged. "First off who are 'we'?"

"Me and Digger."

"Who?"

"Digger." He tutted. "Owen Trench. We all call him Digger, cos, you know, you dig trenches. See?" He went back to pleading. "But we didn't do nowt."

"All right. Undo the knot in your boxer shorts." I took another wet of tea while he stared glumly into his cola. "What were you doing in town that early? On your way to school?"

"College. I'm in Haxford Sixth Form College, and yeah, me and Digger, we were on our way there, but after what happened, we cut college for the day, cos we knew plod would be looking for us. They were gonna throw the book at us."

"Take it easy, John. I'm not the police and I'm not accusing you of anything, but you were still inside Benny's when the gun was fired."

He muttered something and looked even more downcast.

"Sorry. I didn't catch that."

"There weren't no gun. It were me and Digger larking about."

I almost spilled my tea. "What?"

For the first time, I saw some of his father's anger in him. "I said—"

"I heard what you said. Now explain."

Perhaps it was my curt tone of voice, but he didn't answer right away. Instead he took a long drink from his glass and sat for another few moments staring into it as if wondering where or how to start, and I recalled some of my police training. There was a time for talking, a time for pushing and a time to shut up and wait. This fell into the latter category.

"See, Benny's got hold of some electrical gear. You know what I mean? Mics, mini-amps, even a coupla keyboards and stuff. And in amongst it he had these megaphones. Digger, he's like, into that kinda stuff, sound effects, and stuff. And he's good, y'know. He can make noises like jet planes, and car engines and all sorts of stuff. So, just for a gag, he grabbed the megaphone, switched it on and made a sound like a gun being fired. That's what everybody heard. And it weren't half loud. They could have heard it in Huddersfield. Benny went bananas. Musta scared him rotten. He came chasing us and we legged it. That's what the filth saw on the street cameras."

Memories of Tuesday morning assailed me. The rush to get to the library knowing I would be late, the heaving jams all over Yorkshire Street, Huddersfield Street, Batley Way, Simon manning the barrier at the corner of the High Street, and then the rumours; armed robbery, terrorism, even Mandy gearing up for a hostage situation. And all the time it was two teenagers fooling about.

And with the memories came the anger. This silly young man realised the trouble he and his friend had caused, the fear he had instilled in people, the cost to local businesses, the immense cost of the police operation. I wanted to take him by the scruff off the neck and march him off to the police station right there and then. Fortunately, he was a lot bigger than me and there was no way I could have done it. I say fortunate because in that moment when my annoyance hit a peak, I had to hold back, and in doing so, the reality of Tuesday morning seeped into my furious brain.

John and Digger did what teenagers do; played the court jesters. The traffic problems, the fear had nothing to do with them. That was down to Paddy Quinn's overreaction. Instead of ordering a significant police presence, sealing off front and rear entry to Benny's waiting for an on-site assessment from, say, Mandy, he gave orders over the phone to close the High Street and created an unholy mess for a lot of people. He was the one responsible for the chaos and the rumours. And with that knowledge, much to John Frogshaw's puzzlement, I laughed.

He wasn't the only one puzzled by my laughter. So were other customers in Terry's, and one or two passing people along the busy aisles.

I drank more tea to sober me up. "All right, John. Let me get this straight. You're saying that when you ran from the shop, Benny was still on his feet?"

"He chased us out. I don't know what happened to him, but it were nowt to do with me and Digger."

"Why didn't you go to the police and tell them what went on?"

"Me dad told me not to cos if I did, they'd blame me for all the mess. Jeez, missus, I was scared. I haven't ever been in trouble with the filth... well, a coupla warnings for being drunk, but that's all. They'd send me to prison and I'm doing A Levels.

I've got exams the year after next." A tear formed in his eye. "I'm not like me dad. I'm smarter than him. It were all a bit of fun, that's all. I can't go… go to…"

"All right. Just calm down." Tearful teenagers, I could handle. I had my share of practice with Simon and his sister when they were going through that phase. "No one is sending you to prison, but we do need to let the police know about this. I'll speak to Mandy Hiscoe for you. She's fair, Mandy. She'll listen. She might chew you out for not coming to them earlier, but unless Benny decides to press charges, it won't go any further, and I know Benny. He won't be bothered enough to drag you into court." I chewed my lip. "It does beg the question, though, what happened to Benny to put him in hospital?"

"I don't know. It weren't us."

I slid my private eye brain into a higher gear. "Was there anyone else in the shop while you were a larking around?"

He shrugged again. "I think so. It were early. You know. Benny had only just opened, but I'm sure there were at least one other punter in there. Dunno who it was though. Some old biddy, I think. I weren't taking any notice cos me and Digger were too busy running for it when Benny caught us."

So what happened to Benny? The question bounced round my head like an echo constantly repeating, never fading, and I guessed that the only person who could answer it was Benny himself.

I focussed on the distraught young man sat with me. "All right, John, here's what we're going to do.

I'll give Mandy Hiscoe a ring and we'll arrange to speak to her. She's a good friend of mine, and I'm sure she'll listen to you. She might give you a warning for not coming forward sooner. If she does, take my advice and accept it. Apologise and you won't hear anything more. How does that sound."

"You're sure?"

"Positive."

He gave me the slightest of nods. I took out my phone and called Mandy. It rang out and rang out and rang out and then cut to her voicemail. "Mandy, it's Chrissy. Give me a ring when you have a minute, please." I cut the call and focussed again on the young Frogshaw. "Looks like we're on hold for the time being. You get about your business, John, and I'll speak to her later, but when she shows up at your dad's farm, speak to her. Okay?"

He nodded and finished his cola. "Thanks, missus."

With him gone, I ordered fresh tea, and rang Huddersfield Royal, only to be told that they would not discuss Mr Barnes's case with anyone but family. All I wanted to know was whether I could visit, but even pretending to be his sister didn't help. They had obviously relied upon the receptionist at The Cottage as a role model. I rang off and instead rang Barry Barnes.

"He'll be home later this afternoon, Chrissy," he told me. "You know where he lives, don't you?"

"If he's still on Fern Avenue, yes. He's only a few streets from me. Do you think he'll speak to me?"

"Can't guarantee that—" He cut away, directing

one of his customers. "On the bottom shelf, luv. You've got it." He came back to me. "Sorry, Chrissy, but we're going hell for leather this morning. Like I say, I can't guarantee he'll be able to tell you anything, but I'm sure he'll be pleased to see you."

"I'll call on my way home, and thanks, Barry."

I tried Mandy again, with the same result, so I sat, brooding over my fresh tea. The time was coming up to twelve noon, and I was back in no woman's land; nothing to do, nowhere to go, other than maybe home, where I could keep Cappy the Cat company, plan my vlog – even though I had no ideas for content and no adequate conclusions on any of the events of the last few days – and hang a strand of tinsel over and round the clock.

I lifted my cup to finish off the tea and as I did so, my phone warbled for attention. Mandy, I thought, but no. It was Kim. Not just Kim, but a distressed Kim.

"Hi, Kim. Whatever is the matter?"

"Alden. They've arrested him again. They found Harry Kepler and Rita Nuffield dead, and they're doing it again, saying Alden's the book thief, and the Graveyard Poisoner."

Chapter Fourteen

It's at such moments that all sorts of not-quite-random thoughts rush round your head. By not-quite-random, I mean random but sort of focussed on the events of the last few days.

I put them to one side for a moment, calmed Kim down and promised I would be back at the library within the next ten minutes. I settled up with Terry, and made my way out of the market, and as I walked, I tried to clear my thinking.

I wondered just how long this would go on. First his wife – which we all but proved he couldn't have done – and now two of the barflies? 'Ludicrous' was the first word that occurred to me, but that didn't cover it. Alden Upley the Graveyard Poisoner? The book thief? Absolute nonsense. But the more I thought about the possibility, the less nonsensical it became. It was a lot less preposterous than the notion of an armed robbery on Benny's Bargain Basement. And although there were aspects of Benny's contretemps which still needed clearing up, the actual 'armed' angle was solved; teenage horseplay.

It was stretching a point, but on the remote chance that Alden did kill his wife, then I could also imagine him shuffling Harry Kepler and Rita off their respective mortal coils, too. He never liked any of the barflies, but he reserved most of his disdain for Kepler and Rita. Evelyn and the barflies, then, were both possible, but what about the other Graveyard Poisoner victims? Did he have any links to them? Had they upset him sometime in the past? And why would he need to steal library books? If he needed to research poisons and what have you, all he had to do was wait until half past four, get Kim out of the building, and do all his research behind locked doors. He had no need to take the books away.

As I passed the front door of our local, small branch of Sainsbury's, I realised that the link between the Graveyard Poisoner and the book thief had never been substantiated. Indeed, I was the only one truly convinced of it, but Kim was there when I made the assertion. Had I, in all innocence, drawn her up a garden path leading to Alden's second arrest as a book thief as well as a murderer? On the other hand, the police had become aware of it. Why?

And a murderer? Not just a murderer but a serial killer? Impossible. Well, maybe not impossible, but highly unlikely. He was a starchy, stick-in-the-mud, anally-retentive, bog-standard, local government officer, the kind of man who never strayed from the straight and narrow of council regulations, and while I couldn't see Haxford Borough Council including the rule, *committing murder during working hours may lead to disciplinary action*, they would almost certainly include diktats on the desecration of municipal areas like cemeteries and crematoria as committed by the Graveyard Poisoner in the placing of Arthur Rumbelow's body.

I tried to think of other, unassuming serial killers, convinced that there were none. By the time I'd reached Pottle's Pet Supplies, I'd already come up with four, so I abandoned that line of deduction.

I reached the library having decided that of the half dozen or so (including Mrs Upley, Kepler and Rita) killings attributed to the Graveyard Poisoner, Upley might just be guilty of three – his lady wife and the barflies – but he was unlikely to be responsible for the others.

A weepy Kim confirmed as much when I met her in my car on the library car park. The building was shut while a police forensic team went through the library with the emphasis on Alden's personal effects, but she had been given permission to leave so she could meet me.

"He didn't do none of it, Chrissy. Not Alden. It's not him. Killing people? Poisoning them? Me, maybe, but not Alden."

I shuddered and advised her, "Whatever you do, don't say that to the police or they'll wall you up and look for evidence that you're the Graveyard Poisoner." I gave her a moment to calm down then invited, "Tell me what happened this morning."

She dabbed at her eyes, and remained silent for a moment, bringing her emotions under control and calling upon her memory.

"Just after you left, Mandy Hiscoe got a call. We didn't know what it was about and she never said. She just said she had to go but she'd be back later, and she rushed out."

I recalled that I'd seen Mandy hurrying to the car park just before John Frogshaw caught up with me, and when she drove out, she had all her lights blazing.

Kim was still talking. "Twenty minutes later Paddy Quinn turned up and arrested Alden. He said they'd found Kepler and Rita dead in the graveyard at Haxford Parish Church. And yesterday, after they found Evelyn, they were searching Alden's place and they'd found some of the missing library books, and that was it. Alden was stunned. He broke down there and then. Sobbing, he was. Just like a little child. But you know what Quinn's like. About as sensitive as a bulldozer. According to him, they were alligator tears—"

"Crocodile tears," I corrected her.

"Yeah well, whatever. The gospel according to Quinn was that Alden wasn't crying because his missus was dead but like Mandy said yesterday, it was because he'd been caught. I told Quinn he had it wrong, but he wouldn't listen and he carted Alden off to the nick on suspicion of murder."

Kim began to cry again and I had a job and a half to soothe her.

When she was calm again, she went on. "It's not him, Chrissy."

Although I couldn't imagine most of what Kim was saying, mainly because I didn't know Alden that well, I nevertheless agreed with her on the issue of his guilt. There was something wrong with it.

As an aside, I felt it was my duty to disabuse her of her godlike opinion. "There are things you don't know about him, Kim," I told her. "I mean that memory stick for a start off—"

"Oh, you mean the mickey mouse films. Course I know about them. Who do you think gave him the web address where to find them?" A look of horror crossed her features. "Oh, my god, the cops have taken that memory stick away. When they see what's on them, he—"

Information was crowding in on me again. "Hold on, hold on. Just slow down a minute. When you gave me that memory stick, you said you didn't know what the other videos were."

"Cos I didn't. Well, not really. What I actually said was, I didn't know what they were because I didn't have time to look at them."

It was thin, but because of her distress I accepted her excuse even though it was much more likely that she assumed I wouldn't look at them. "Yes, well, be that as it may, owning that kind of, er filth is not illegal, and if it spells out some flaw in his character, it still doesn't make him a murderer." I could feel a frown coming on. "How come you gave him the website address? I mean, did he ask you outright?"

"Nah, did he heck as like. It must be… what… two years ago now, maybe longer. He came in one morning seriously depressed. He was late opening up and that's not like Alden. I asked what was up and he wouldn't tell me. Eventually, he admitted it was problem with his wife, so I pushed him a bit further. He went all red in the face when he told me." Kim gave a tearful laugh at the memory. "I told him, I said, 'get yourself a bit on the side', but he said he couldn't do that to Evelyn." Now suddenly she was pleading again. "He really loved her, Chrissy, but he wasn't getting enough, er, of the other. So I gave him a couple of web addresses where he could download the necessary."

My thinking was becoming clouded again. "Don't take this the wrong way, Kim, but are you sure there isn't more to you and Alden than you're telling me?"

"Nothing. I might not have objected, but he would."

I took that to mean that she had flashed inviting eyes at him and he'd frozen her out. "But you encouraged him to visit… er, adult sites."

"I was trying to help, Chrissy. I don't go to those sites, but my fella, Wayne – you remember him. The rotten sod who walked out on me. Anyway, he was into that kinda stuff when I first met him. I mean, most blokes are, aren't they?"

Thinking automatically about my other half, I had to disagree with her. "Not my Dennis. His idea of a stripper is someone taking an old car to pieces." The discussion was drifting along a side track and we needed to get it back where it belonged. "Did the police say how long Kepler and Rita had been dead?"

"No. They reckon he must have killed them last night or first thing this morning, just like he was supposed to have done with Evelyn, but Alden didn't leave my place last night, and we came to work together this morning. He gave me a lift."

It was like somebody switched on the light. It was so obvious, and if he didn't kill Harry Kepler, then what price…

I stemmed the flow of realisation which threatened to swamp me. "What are you up to now, Kim?"

"I've gotta stay until the library's official closing time. We won't be opening again today, but I have make sure those thieving coppers don't help themselves to books, newspapers and stuff. No offence, Chrissy. I know you were a copper and I wasn't including your Simon."

I reassured her again, and as she climbed out, I took out my phone and rang Mandy. No answer.

For the second time in as many days, I battled my way to the police station, had another argument with Minx before Paddy came storming out of the interview rooms.

"What is it with you? Can't you leave us to get on with the job we're paid to do?"

"When you learn how to do it, maybe I will," I snapped. Forcing calm upon myself, I told him, "Alden is innocent. He didn't kill Kepler and Rita Nuffield."

"Again? He was innocent yesterday, too, wasn't he?"

"I saw Kepler and Rita getting out of Patience Shuttle's van on the library car park. That was at about ten past nine this morning. Alden was already in the library and he didn't leave the building until you blundered in and arrested him. For God's sake, Paddy, he was still there when you came in reading us the riot act about the Graveyard Poisoner and the stolen books. He couldn't have killed them."

He turned on me again. "He's still guilty of nicking those books."

"Talk sense."

"His dabs are all over them."

"Of course they are. He runs the library. And I'll bet they're covered in other prints. Get your brain in gear, Paddy. Why would he steal books from the library when he could read them during his tea break? You've got the wrong man."

At first he began to sweat, but then, a slow smile crept across his face. "Yeah, but you don't know what we found on one of his memory sticks."

"I've seen those videos so I know exactly what you found, and while I don't necessarily approve, you know as well as I do that possession of that kind of material is not illegal, as long as he's not selling it. Even then, I'm not so sure in this day and age. Face it, Paddy, you jumped the gun... again; just like you did when you shut the High Street on Tuesday."

The sweat was more profuse now and the noisome odour began to get to me. "I did not jump the gun on Tuesday. It was an armed incident."

"It was two teenagers fooling around with a megaphone."

At that point, I wondered how many more shocks he could take without succumbing to a heart attack, and I held my phone ready to dial 999 if I had to, although Minx would probably beat me to it.

"What? What did you say about the business in Barnes's place?"

He wasn't the only one on the point of losing it. My frustration was beginning to get the better of me too. I mentally counted to three. "Send someone out to Frogshaw's farm and speak to young John. I spent the better part of an hour with him this morning and he told me exactly what happened in Benny's. There was no gun. It was him and Owen Trench acting the goat with a megaphone."

"Before they beat Benny up. I'll bet."

"According to young Froggy, Benny chased them out of the shop. You got it wrong again, Paddy. Now let Alden go, and get statements from the leads I've given you and with a bit of luck, we'll see you clear off back to Huddersfield and get some peace in Haxford before Christmas."

He came back on the front foot. "Not while the Graveyard Poisoner is out there." He aimed a shaking finger at me. "Right now, I want to know everything you know."

As before, he left it to Mandy who assured me that officers had been dispatched to Patience Shuttle's place and the Frogshaws' farm.

"Paddy jumping the gun again," she admitted to me. "It's what comes of listening to Patience."

That was problematic from my point of view. "Patience Shuttle? What does she have to do with anything?"

"She lives round the corner from Upley, doesn't she? Her and her sisters. Greenmount Terrace. She came wandering past when we set to work in the parish church yard, and said to Paddy, 'That'll please Alden Upley.' When Paddy asked why, Patience told him about Upley banning Kepler from the library... yesterday, was it? That was enough for Paddy. He ordered me back to the station and shot off down to the library and the next thing we knew, Alden was arrested on suspicion... for the second time."

Suspicion also began to haunt me again. "How did Patience know what you'd found in the churchyard? I mean, you usually put up a shroud to keep nosy parkers out, don't you? Your people didn't talk, did they?"

Another sigh. "Probably. If not, it's the bush telegraph, isn't it? One of them gets the drift, calls at the shops, and ten minutes later, it's spread like kennel cough going through a dog's home." She let out a sigh. "We're still speaking to Alden, but we'll let him go later. In the meantime, young Frogshaw should have come to us on Tuesday morning about the business in Benny's."

"I told him that, but he was scared, Mandy. Scared that Paddy would lock him up and throw the key away. And you and I both know that's exactly how Paddy would have reacted."

She sighed. "You're probably right. He was the same this morning when he hauled Alden in. I warned him he was jumping the gun, but he wouldn't listen. When does he ever?"

I came out of the police station a tumult of different emotions and opinions. Time, I decided, to put it all out of my mind and speak to Benny Barnes, but when I rang Barry, he told me his father wasn't yet home. He promised to get Benny to ring me late that afternoon, so I called in at Warrington's and from there, made my way home.

Chapter Fifteen

Cappy the Cat was delighted to see me, but only because the little tyke knew I was carrying cream cakes.

Half an hour later, I'd had a rest, Cappy the Cat was polishing off what remained of the goodies, and it was time to get on, but I was torn between the tedium of research, necessary if I was to put a vlog out this side of Christmas, and the excitement of tarting up the house in time for that same Christmas. Should I strain to make sense of the inquiries I was making, or put lights in the windows of the china cottage. A tough decision, but ultimately, the cottage won the day. I'd been neglecting my Christmas decorations over the last three days.

The cottage was a charming little piece, hand-painted according to the label. It sported redbrick walls, with holes where the windows were supposed to be, a painted on, old-fashioned wooden door, and a snow-covered roof. I bought it from a stall on a Christmas market in Leeds, and I think I paid about five pounds for it. That was a couple of years back. I really enjoyed that Saturday afternoon, and Dennis came away with a smile on his face, too, after some busty young German girl sold him a torque wrench set. She may have imagined he was switched on by her charms, most of which were on display beneath a tiny, tight-fitting costume, but I knew my husband better. Her ample breasts and shapely legs were no match for a torque-wrench set priced at less than ten pounds.

"Normally, I can't find one of these for less than a score," he told me as we came away from the market. He was less impressed six months later when some of the interchangeable sockets began to 'round off'. "Cheap Chinese junk," he grumbled.

Teasing the tea lights into the cottage through the gaps in the back of the ornament was difficult, but eventually I had them where I wanted, and I placed it under the telly, then stood back to admire the affect. Perfect. It would be a bit of a nuisance taking the tea lights out to switch them on of an evening, but I was sure it would be worth it.

I opened the cotton wool balls and got down on my knees to begin moulding them together and spreading them along the lower shelf of the smoked glass TV table, and I was not a quarter of the way through the job when my phone rang. It was Benny's wife, telling me he was home and if I wanted to visit, he'd be happy to see me.

I dressed for the weather again, climbed into the car and drove to the end of the street where instead of turning left for town, I turned right, up the hill, and took the next right, onto Gorse Road and the first left into Fern Avenue.

It could have been a twin of Bracken Close. The two-bed bungalows were the same as ours, with a few sporting the dormer to create a third bedroom, something we already had. The doors and windows had the same appearance, from which I always guessed some double glazing salesman must have made a major killing at some point in time. Front and rear gardens, up and over garages all looked as if they could have been uprooted from our street. It was modern suburbia and heaven to anyone with a craving to conform.

Benny's wife let me in, offered me tea, which I declined, and left me alone to talk to her husband in the living room.

He looked very sorry for himself seated in an armchair facing the TV, a travel blanket wrapped round his knees and a bandage wrapped round his head. In fact, he looked old, frail and weak, and yet, I knew for a fact that he was only a year or so younger than me, and early fifties is no age for travel blankets and head bandages.

"It's good of you to come, Christine," he said in a tiny voice. He even sounded old and frail.

"I told the woman at The Cottage that I'm one of your best customers, Benny, and I couldn't settle without seeing you. Plus, all my viewers will want to know how you're getting on."

"I'll be all right... eventually. Our Barry's having to do all the hard work right now."

"That's what sons are for." I took a look around the room, wondering where to go next. Amongst the Christmas decorations, there was an array of get well cards on the mantelpiece, and I mentally smacked my legs. Why hadn't I bought him one? I'm never backward when it comes to greetings cards.

Eventually, I bit the bullet. "What actually

happened, Benny? You'd never believe the rumours floating about. Everything from a major, armed heist, to a full blown terrorist attack."

"Twaddle," he said. "All of it. There weren't no guns. It was two kids larking about with some of the electrical stuff I bought. I chased the little so and so's out." A frown crossed his faces. "There were other people in the shop though and I can't remember who or what they wanted. Rita Nuffield was one… I think. Patience Shuttle, oh and I can't be sure, but I think that friend of yours, Kim Aspinall. I think she was there."

"She was on a bus, Benny. She couldn't get to town for the traffic jam."

"Oh. There you are then. The doctors told me my memory might be a bit hazy for a while."

"So how did you come to black out?"

"Well, that's it, you see. I can't remember. What I do remember is a clout on the back of the neck and after that…" He shrugged. "Nothing. According to them in the know, I fell backwards and banged my head against the edge of a shelf. That's what gave me concussion."

"But you are on the mend?"

"Oh, aye I'll be back in the shop before you know it. I'll just take a few days off over Christmas, and then I'll be there." He gave me a weak smile. "Just in case you need a new dustpan and brush for t'New Year."

I spent another half hour with him, reminiscing over days gone by (I had known him many, many years) and then as the darkness began to descend, I got back in my car and drove home.

Cappy the Cat was pleased to see me, but only because he wanted feeding. That is one greedy little cat. No sooner had he wolfed down a dishful and checked his territory outside, than he was curled up and ignoring everything and everyone again.

Something was bothering me, and it was not something I had just learned... Correction. It was something I'd just learned, but it meshed with everything else that had happened over the last three days. And it was something trivial, something which might escape other people, and as I focussed my mind, I realised it might just escape me too.

Was it a some*thing* or some*one*? I didn't know and my brain wouldn't unlock far enough for me to narrow it down.

The decoration-less clock told me it as coming up to four o'clock. I moved to the workstation, switched on the laptop and with a fresh cup of tea within reach, I noted down everything that had happened, everything I had learned since Tuesday.

Benny attacked, traffic jam, Upley's stolen books, Mandy pregnant, Evelyn dead, mini-camera damaged by Harry Kepler, Upley's naughty films, potential link to the Graveyard Poisoner, John Frogshaw, Harry's sudden death, Upley arrested, Benny's amnesia... and that was it.

That was it?

Surely more than that had happened? When I thought about it, that was the sum total of my learning, and the only repetition was the mention of Alden Upley, but he was in the clear. I'd cleared him. In a mood of despair, I reappraised my reappraisal of my prowess as a private investigator.

I was rubbish.

The phone rang. Staring at the laptop screen, I picked it up, absently registered Kim's name on the phone and made connection. "Hi, Kim. What's up, luv?"

She was so distressed, she practically screamed into the phone. "It's Alden. He's tried to kill himself."

I forgot all about the laptop. "What? What are you talking about?"

"Patience Shuttle just told me. When the police released him, he went into CutCost, bought a pack of sixteen paracetamol tablets and a bottle of water, and swallowed the lot in one go while he was in the supermarket. Security tried to stop him, but he pushed them away."

"Never mind listening to Patience Shuttle," I said. "Have you confirmed this?"

"Course I have. I spoke to Mandy and she said it was spot on. They've rushed him to Huddersfield. Stomach pump job, I reckon."

"It'll be too late for that, but there are ways of neutralising it. That's what they'll do. Make sure it doesn't hit his kidneys and liver."

"What's happening to this town, Chrissy? It's gone crackers."

"I know, Kim, I know. You just keep calm, and worry about yourself, not Alden Upley."

I took me another five minutes to persuade her, and all the while bells were ringing at the back of my mind, and when I finally cut the call, I knew. I knew exactly what, or rather who, I had been missing.

It would take me most of the evening to go through the entire raft of events and firm up what I knew. Dennis was not bothered. When he'd had his tea, he found Bullit repeating on some digital channel, and he was quite happy to sit and watch that.

By eleven o'clock, I was certain. Putting in an appearance everywhere, spending a long time priming Kepler and Rita in the library, pronouncing judgement on Evelyn Upley, even asking after the investigation, it had to be, it just had to be.

And yet, there was no proof and I was only going to close the case in one way. I would have to come face to face with the Graveyard Poisoner.

Chapter Sixteen

As Dennis prepared to leave for work, I handed him two Christmas cards. "One for Tony and one for Lester. The envelopes are marked."

He tutted. "We have this same palaver every year, it's not right me giving 'em Christmas cards. Men don't do that kinda stuff."

"With stamps costing something like seventy pence each, I refuse to drop them in the post. Not while you work with them. Just hand them over when you get to work, Dennis, and stop arguing."

"You make me look a right ruddy fool."

"Take it from me, you don't need any help in that department."

He went off to work and I prepared myself for what I had to do. I hadn't told Dennis. He'd have made himself late for work trying to talk me out of it (yes, there were times when other things mattered to him more than engines and his business). I'd spent half the night working this out, and if I could have seen any alternative, I would have taken it. But there was none. The police would never prove it, the Graveyard Poisoner would never confess to them, so it was this or nothing.

Mandy, too, was dead set against it. "You're putting yourself at risk, Chrissy," she told me when

I put my conclusions to her at nine o'clock."

"I'm aware of that, but I'm sure I can handle it… or them. All you need to do, Mandy is stand by, and wait for my text."

"And what if you're wrong? What if it isn't—"

"Then one of us will be made to look a fool and Paddy Quinn will do an Irish jig and ask you to marry him when he gets to know it's me. Everything fits, but it's all circumstantial and the margin of error is too great. That's why it has to be me, not you. I may be able to get a confession. You never would."

She clucked like a mother hen. "When I say 'what if you're wrong', I'm not just thinking about you. If you're wrong and Paddy finds out I knew what you were doing—"

"He will never get to know," I interrupted for the second time. "Not from me, anyway."

"Oh, for God's sake. If anything happens to you, I… I'll never speak to you again."

"I take that as a given," I said and rang off.

The clock, still minus its decoration, read half past nine. I gave Cappy the Cat a cuddle he didn't want, and followed that by spoiling him with the leftovers of another cream cake which he did want, and then locked up and climbed into the car. Nervous? I was trembling so much I struggled to get the key in the ignition.

It was a drive of not much more than ten minutes. Up above a dark sky grumbled its way across the moors and the town, threatening more snow, and I pondered the possibility of a true, white Christmas. "It's all right on Christmas cards, calendars, and adverts on the telly," Dennis would often say, "but in reality it's a flaming nightmare. Especially when you have to go out and rescue some banana who gets stuck in it."

Right now, my biggest worry was whether I would see it or not, and I automatically recalled my days on the force when we were called out to situations which were not exactly life-threatening, but certainly hazardous. That's how I viewed the forthcoming confrontation. Back then, of course, we had back up. We went out *en masse*; never less than six or twelve-handed. All officers were trained not to go into such situations alone. Hadn't Paddy Quinn chewed Mandy out for doing exactly that when she walked into Benny's Bargain Basement at the height of the theoretical siege on Tuesday morning? And hadn't Mandy just chewed me out for proposing the same thing, and wasn't I taking the same attitude as she had? Any other course of action would be doomed to failure, and if I didn't confront it, how many more innocent people would die?

I reminded myself that this was not a Saturday night ruck outside the Weavers. This would be a one to one, or maybe one to three and if I had the advantage of a younger age, they were in a position where they could see me coming and prepare. I was walking into unknown territory.

Mandy's car was parked, engine running, outside the Upleys' when I passed and turned up Greenmount Terrace. She was sat at the wheel and I gave her a wave as I drove by. She did not acknowledge me, but dropped in behind as I carried on up the short cul-de-sac. Twice I tried to wave her back, twice she ignored me, and when I pulled up at the bottom of their drive, she pulled past and blocked their potential exit.

I climbed out of the car. "What do you think you're doing?"

She numbered both items on her fingers. "One, making sure they don't try to do a runner, and two, making sure you don't get your head caved in or a stomach full of strychnine."

"Mandy—"

For once it was her turn to interrupt me. "Just shut up, Chrissy, and use your nut. I can see the sense in everything you've told me, but I guarantee they will deny it whether you're alone or with me. I also guarantee that they will offer you – and me – a cuppa, and that could just be all I need. And while I think on, if they do offer, don't drink it."

The houses were older than those on Greenmount Lane, large, stone built, with ample gardens at the front and I guessed spreads just as large at the back. The old Morris van stood on the drive, and as we walked up to the side door, I noticed a large flowerbed at the edge of the back garden. Nothing surprising about that perhaps, but it was raised at least eighteen inches above what appeared to be the general level of the garden. My suspicions strengthened. I knew the secret of that flowerbed… or at least, I persuaded myself that I knew,

Mandy knocked on the door and many seconds passed before Patience opened it.

"Sergeant Hiscoe. This is a surprise. And

Christine Capper. What do you want?"

"A brief word, Ms Shuttle," Mandy said. "May we come in?"

"Of course, but we'll have to keep the noise down. The twins are still in bed. Asleep."

Were they, I asked myself? I hoped they were.

She let us in through a kitchen which was not just old but ancient. My parents had lived most of their married life in a two up two down terraced place, but even my mother's kitchen was better appointed than this. Patience had an old gas stove of the kind before pilot lights and white enamel were invented. There was no fridge, only a brace of freestanding crockery/larder cupboards, and the sink was made of white stone stood on four legs. Worse, all the pipes leading to it were on display. On the wall hung several cooking/baking tools, amongst which I noticed a wooden meat mallet, the kind alleged to have struck Arthur Rumbelow on the back of the head. I checked through the rear window, looking out on the back garden, and learned that there was not one but no less than three raised flowerbeds. My heart began to pound. Another suspicion realised? Surely not... she couldn't have... could she? I knew then that she had.

She led us into a gloomy living room and once again I had the impression of passing through some kind of time warp. The carpet was older than me, threadbare and dirty, in need of some serious Dyson attention. But it didn't look as if it could stand anything as powerful as the Dyson. Maybe a Bex Bissell then. In the hearth of an old, black fireplace, the kind my grandma used to treat with black lead every week, stood a small gas fire, its four tubular radiants throwing out meagre heat. In the corner by the window was a teeny television set, which surely dated back to the 1960s, and which probably showed only black and white pictures. Focussed upon it was a deep seated suite, consisting of settee and two matching armchairs, all of them upholstered in dark, brown leather, cracked and frayed in places, the seams outlined by black studs.

Patience waved us to the settee and asked, "Would you like some tea?"

With Mandy's warning in mind I was about to refuse, but the sergeant got there before me. "I'd luv a cuppa. Milk and no sugar, please."

Patience shuffled back to the kitchen and we could hear her filling the kettle, lighting the gas, preparing cups.

A silent conversation passed between Mandy and me, consisting mostly of small gestures and accompanying facial expressions, best summed up as me asking, 'What are you playing at?' and Mandy replying, 'Trust me, I know what I'm doing.' My response to that was a half scowl which read, 'If you know what you're doing, I'll run my knickers up the town hall flagpole.'

Soon, we heard the whistle of the kettle, a sound I hadn't heard since the days when I used to go to my gran's after school to wait for my mum coming home from work. Then Patience, carrying a tray with three beakers on it, joined us.

"No cups and saucers here, I'm afraid. I've never been one to stand on ceremony."

She lowered the tray and for a moment I thought she was going to drop it. She didn't and for an even shorter moment, I was tempted to tip it up out of her hands, but Mandy got there first and took two of the beakers, passing one to me. Patience lifted the last one, dropped the tray alongside her chair, sat down and took a healthy swig from the beaker. "Ah, that's better. Nowt like a good cuppa, is there?"

I murmured my agreement and Mandy nodded, but neither of us drank.

"So, what can I do for you?" Patience took another large swallow of tea and I guessed she must have a mouth lined with asbestos. I was nursing my beaker on my lap, and I could feel the heat getting to my skin three layers down.

Mandy nudged me and I almost spilled the tea. I cleared my throat. "I know it all, Patience. The first four victims, Oscar, Arthur, George, Herbert, then Evelyn Upley, Rita Nuffield, Harry Kepler, clouting Benny Barnes, stealing those books from the library. I know it was all you."

"Ah. I see."

In that moment, I knew I had it right. If I was wrong, she would have come back with something like, 'what was me' but she didn't.

"The only thing is, I'm not sure why."

To my surprise, and I think Mandy's, Patience laughed. "You know, there are times when I ask myself the same question, and I'm not always sure of the answer. I can tell you why Harry and Rita and why Evelyn."

But I knew part of that already. "Harry and Rita helped you, didn't they?"

She nodded. "They did. But when you started to get nosy and I asked Harry to rip down that camera of yours, they lost what little bit of guts they had and they were threatening to grass me up unless I handed over a lot of money I don't have. Idiots. Course, they weren't involved in any of the killing. They just helped me shift the leftovers, get the bodies to the churchyards and stuff. They didn't think they'd done anything wrong. Like I said, idiots. And then to try and blackmail me?"

"So you invited them to enjoy a cup of tea?" Mandy asked.

"A beer, actually. Rita wolfed it down but Harry was more cautious. When she fell to the carpet choking, he'd already taken a small swallow of beer, and it dawned on him. When he started coughing, too, he tried to get it all back up, but I pinched his nose and tipped it down his throat. Took him, what? No more than ten minutes to clock out." She shook her ageing head. "It was a bad 'un, that. I didn't have time to prepare them, wash him or anything, I had to get them down to t'Parish Church while it were cold and people were inside, out of the way."

"Why plant the library books on Alden?"

"I didn't. I planted them on Evelyn. It never occurred to me that the police would blame Alden. It's a stupid idea. He ran the library. Why would he steal books? But she might. Just to spite him."

"And she was chosen a long time ago, wasn't she?" I said.

"I did it for Alden. That poor man had suffered long enough. He deserved better." Patience glared a challenge at me. "I told you that t'other day." The challenge shifted to Mandy. "And I told your bobbies summat like the same thing when they were searching their house."

I shook my head in an effort to control my irritation. "You ruined his life, Patience. For all her faults, Alden loved her."

"No. He only thinks he did. Now that he's widowed, he'll find someone else, and he'll be a lot happier for it."

I couldn't hold it in any longer. "For your information, after the police questioned him about Kepler and Rita, he took an overdose of paracetamol last night. He's in hospital."

I might have said nothing for all Patience cared. "I know. I was there in CutCost when he did it. He's a bigger wimp than I thought."

"He loved her, Patience," I repeated. "But that's a word you don't understand, isn't it?"

"Happen you're right. Happen I don't. But I told you he deserved better."

It was left to Mandy to bring us back on track. "You started about two years ago, Patience. Why? What was it about those men?"

"Simple enough. They were lonely. They'd lived a long time and had lives which amounted to nothing. I put it right for them. Oscar Longwood, widowed, crabby. I solved his problem for him. Arthur Rumbelow, widowed, lonely. Well, he isn't any longer. George Dalston, pansy, wandering from man to man trying to find true love. He doesn't have that trouble now. Herbie Pickles, same as the others; widowed, didn't know what to do with himself, so I sorted it out for him." Her gaze rested on both of us. "I did the decent thing by 'em. A bit of rough embalming – our Bob worked for a funeral director once over, and he told me what embalming were all about. I had to be sneaky in the cemeteries, but I laid 'em out proper on the graves. I even said prayers for them. It were a kindness. I was doing them all a favour because I knew what they were going through."

My suspicions homed in on the bullseye. "And you became lonely after you killed Robert, Faith and Charity, didn't you?"

Mandy's eyes opened wide, but Patience chuckled. "You're a clever one, Christine Capper. Don't let no one tell you different. How did you work it out?"

"Just now when I saw your back garden though the kitchen window. Nobody's seen hide nor hair of Bob for years, and it occurred to me that no one's seen anything of the twins either. We only assumed they were alive because you talked about them now and then. Just now I saw three flower beds all raised and just about the right size for a body. It was obvious."

She began to cough and it took her a minute to get it under control. "It's three year since. They were at it. Bob, Faith and Charity. All three of 'em in t'same bed. His fault, I think. I mean he did it to me when I were younger. Dirty little toe rag. I were nowt but a young girl and I didn't really know what he was doing or what it meant. I soon found out, mind, and I warned him never to come near me again and he didn't. But those two. I think they enjoyed it. Anyway, I got supper ready that night, hit 'em all with a good dose of strychnine. Took me three nights to get rid of 'em in the back garden." She glared defiance. "They deserved it. All of 'em."

Mandy cottoned on. "And you carried on claiming their pensions?"

Patience began coughing again. Her breath was coming in short gasps. "Well, no death certificates cos no one knew they were dead, and the beauty of pensions today is they're paid straight into t'bank, and we had a joint account. Been like that for years. Shared between the four of us. Their pensions and mine kept me in custard powder."

Mandy had heard enough, but I had outstanding questions. "How did you manage to move the bodies, Patience? I mean, I know you had Harry and Rita help you, but how did you get them to the graveyards?"

"Trolley and a ramp in the back of the van. I had to be careful, mind. We got seen once over, but the cops never made anything of it. Thought it were some funeral director shifting bodies to his chapel of rest." She gave a gleeful chuckle.

"Where did you get the strychnine?" Mandy wanted to know "It's a controlled substance."

"See, that's the trouble with you young'uns. You know nowt. When I were a girl, you could buy it, if you knew where to go. We used it as rat poison, and the old man, he got plenty of it in." She gestured round at the room. "Old place like this, haven for rats it were. Still is. Course, I didn't know how effective it'd be. It'd been down in the cellar for years. So I gave 'em plenty." She cackled. "All of 'em."

Another coughing fit overtook her, and my suspicions swung in another direction. "Benny's? You ran out of strychnine, didn't you?"

"Not quite. I needed a top up but like you said, you can't get it any more. So I went for some weedkiller. Glyphosate." She laughed and coughed. "I got that name from one of them library books I took. I guessed that Benny's was the only place I could get it without people asking too many questions, but he wouldn't sell me half a dozen boxes, so I clattered him with me walking stick and when he fell, he caught his head on one of the shelves. With him out of it, I walked out the back door with all the weedkiller I wanted." She pointed at our beakers. "Here, come on drink your tea. I haven't put nowt in it, you know."

"You think either of us would trust you?" Mandy asked.

Patience began to cough more violently, her breathing was short, raspy, struggling, and the truth hit me.

"I think she's telling us the truth," I ventured. "You've used it all up, haven't you, Patience?"

"Aye, lass. I have." For a moment, she held up her beaker, and then let it fall to the dirty carpet. And she fell after it.

***

We sat in Mandy's car, drinking coffee from her thermos. Neither of us had touched the tea Patience made. I believed her when she said she had put nothing in it, but Mandy wasn't prepared to let either of us take the chance.

After checking and confirming that Patience was either dead or so close that medics would make no difference, Mandy put in a call to them anyway, and then rang Quinn, to give him the overview, and from there we made our way out to her car.

In less than a quarter of an hour, the little street was swarming with police vehicles and a couple of paramedics who, after declaring Patience dead, went on their way, leaving it to pathology and forensics. By the time Paddy arrived, a team were already digging up the back garden, and the white, scientific support van had begun to fill up with seal-easy boxes, taking away such evidence as would need logging and analysing.

Paddy had a screaming fit for not telling him in advance, I told him where to go and so did Mandy, but she used language a lot stronger than I like to hear from a young woman, especially one due to become a mother.

"A sad and vicious old woman," Mandy declared as we sipped our coffee.

"I don't think she was vicious," I said. "Callous, certainly, and totally misguided, but the only malice was in murdering Evelyn Upley. Kepler and Rita were, sort of, self-preservation."

"And yet she topped herself."

"That was probably because we showed up, Mandy. She knew it was all over."

Mandy abruptly changed the subject. "You know you can't say anything about this on your vlog, don't you?"

"Not until you've cleared it all up," I replied.

"And then I'll clue my viewers up. You never know, I might increase my audience and then I can jack up my sponsorship price."

She laughed. "Yorkshire through and through." Then she sighed. "Dear me. What a mess."

"Look on the bright side."

She cocked a quizzical eye at me. "Is there one?"

"Oh, yes. You'll get rid of Paddy Quinn in time for Christmas."

Mandy laughed and I got out of the car.

"Have a good Christmas, Mandy."

"And you, Chrissy, and you."

Epilogue

And that's the whole story.

Christmas morning dawned but it wasn't a white Christmas. There were some odd patches of snow, hangovers of the last few days, tucked away against the bottom of garden walls and under hedgerows, and the sky was still mucky enough to deliver a drop more before the day was out. It was cold, though, as Cappy the Cat let us know when he shot out of the house at half past eight and was back in front of the fire by twenty-five to nine.

Dennis was up just after six, as always, and I was about two hours behind him. No rest for the wicked. Not in this house. Not when we were expecting guests in the middle of the afternoon.

A lot happened after the business at the Shuttles' place the previous morning. Paddy Quinn called just after twelve noon and apologised for the way he had put me down on Thursday. He also thanked me for my efforts in confronting Patience, but never one to let matters go without a token moan, he also told me how reckless it was. He'd said the same thing to Mandy apparently.

I accepted all this with good grace.

Ingrid rang at two o'clock saying she had fallen out with her boyfriend and could she come home for Christmas. I told her she could. What else would I do? I was looking forward to seeing her, having a good few mother and daughter natters when she rang back at four o'clock and told me to scratch it. She and her boyfriend had kissed and made up.

Kim rang late in the afternoon as I was preparing everything for the forthcoming feast. Alden had been discharged from hospital and he would be staying with her for Christmas.

"He can't bear to be in his house," she explained.

Dennis started the day by complaining about having to deliver the Christmas cards to Lester and Tony, and as a punishment, I made him hang the tinsel round the clock. The next thing I saw was him at the top of the stepladder measuring the wall above the clock. "You want it equal on both sides, woman," he told me, "and to do that, I need a centre line." When I protested that he was taking things too far, I got the standard, 'if a job's worth doing, it's worth doing right,' response. A job I'm sure I could have done in less than ten minutes took him the better part of half an hour, but it looked acceptable.

I managed to put out a short, Christmassy vlog assuring my viewers that Haxford was back to normal. Benny would soon recover, Alden Upley was on the mend, and all was right with the world.

But in between these flurries of activity, I couldn't help reflecting on the last few days, and with that came feelings of guilt. If I hadn't put up that spy camera, would Harry Kepler still be alive and scrounging beer, cigarettes, and money where he could? If I'd realised the omnipresence of

Patience Shuttle earlier, would Evelyn Upley still be with us? It's nothing more than speculation, but I can't help that little twinge of regret now and then that I didn't think or move fast enough.

The Graveyard Poisoner is history now. Haxford is back amongst the small potatoes in the world of crime but there was one thing I never cleared up.

A month later, Kim moved in with Alden Upley at his house. They're not ready for calling the banns. It's far too soon after Evelyn's death but it did pose another question.

A couple of times over that week, I'd wondered whether there was anything between Kim and Alden. I still don't know, but I don't think so. He was far too starchy for an affair, but Kim's distress at his arrest and his attempted suicide led me to conclude that she'd been carrying a torch for him for some time.

He's ten years older than her – give or take – but during Evelyn's funeral, I learned that she was five years older than Alden, so maybe things will work out.

And now you know the whole truth about the run up to Christmas here in Haxford, and that, my friends, concludes this special edition of Christine Capper's Comings and Goings. I'll see you next time.

THE END

THANK YOU FOR READING. I HOPE YOU HAVE ENJOYED THIS BOOK. WOULD YOU BE KIND ENOUGH TO LEAVE A RATING OR REVIEW ON AMAZON?

The Author

David W Robinson retired from the rat race after the other rats objected to his participation, and he now lives with his long-suffering wife in sight of the Pennine Moors outside Manchester.

Best known as the creator of the light-hearted and ever-popular **Sanford 3rd Age Club Mysteries**, and in the same vein, **Mrs Capper's Casebook**. He also produces darker, more psychological crime thrillers as in the **Feyer & Drake** thrillers and occasional standalone titles.

He, produces his own videos, and can frequently be heard grumbling against the world on Facebook at https://www.facebook.com/davidrobinsonwriter/ and has a YouTube channel at https://www.youtube.com/user/Dwrob96/videos.
For more information you can track him down at www.dwrob.com and if you want to sign up to my newsletter and pick up a #FREE book or two, you can find all the details at https://dwrob.com/readers-club/

By the same Author
Mrs Capper's Casebook

Christine Capper is a solid, down to earth Yorkshire lass, witty, plain spoken, but with an innate sense of inquiry (all right, then, she's nosy). She passes her days in the West Yorkshire town of Haxford looking after her long-suffering husband, Dennis, a man with an obsession for all things automotive, and putting him right when he goes wrong, which is more often than not. She takes care of their pet, Cappy the Cat, a feline with attitude, dotes on her granddaughter Bethany, and is openly proud of her son, Simon, now Acting Detective Constable Capper of the Haxford force.

A former police officer, she's Haxford's only trained and licenced private investigator. She's choosy about the cases she takes on but appears destined to be dragged into more serious affairs, during which she passes on her findings to her friend, Detective Sergeant Mandy Hiscoe and Mandy's immediate boss, DI Paddy Quinn, a man who is quite open about his dislike for private eyes.

A series of light-hearted mysteries, laced with Yorkshire grit and wit, Mrs Capper's Casebooks are exclusive to Amazon available for the Kindle and in paperback.

You can find them at:
https://mybook.to/cappseries

The Sanford 3rd Age Club Mysteries

These titles are published and managed by Darkstroke Books

A decade on from their debut, there are 26 volumes (soon to be 27) and a special in the Sanford 3rd Age Club Mystery series.

We follow the travels and trials of amateur sleuth Joe Murray and his two best friends, Sheila Riley and Brenda Jump. The short, irascible Joe, proprietor of The Lazy Luncheonette in Sanford, West Yorkshire, jollied along by the bubbly Brenda and Sheila, but only his friends, but also his employees, all three leading lights in the Sanford 3rd Age Club (STAC for short). And it seems that wherever they go on their outings on holidays in the company of the born-again teenagers of the 3rd Age Club, they bump into… MURDER.

A major series of whodunits marinated in Yorkshire humour, they are exclusive to Amazon and you can find them at: **https://mybook.to/stac**

Other Works

I also turn out darker works such as The Anagramist and The Frame with Chief Inspector Samantha Feyer and civilian consultant Wesley Drake, and the standalone The Cutter.

For details visit https://dwrob.com/the-dark/

Free Books

Like what you've seen so far? Why to subscribe to my newsletter? I guaranteed that you will not be inundated with emails, and your address will never be sold on. Once you sign up, you will receive details of to one but TWO free novellas.

For more information visit
https://dwrob.com/readers-club/

Printed in Great Britain
by Amazon